Ba

Saints Among Us

Tales from Grace Chapel Inn

Saints Among Us

ANNE MARIE RODGERS

Guideposts
New York, New York

Saints Among Us

ISBN-13: 978-0-8249-4826-9

Published by Guideposts
16 East 34th Street
New York, New York 10016
www.guideposts.com

Distributed by Ideals Publications, a Guideposts company
2630 Elm Hill Pike, Suite 100
Nashville, TN 37214

Library of Congress Cataloging-in-Publication Data

Rodgers, Anne Marie.
    Saints among us / Anne Marie Rodgers.
       p. cm. — (Tales from Grace Chapel Inn)
    ISBN 978-0-8249-4826-9
    1. Bed and breakfast accommodations—Fiction.   2. Pennsylvania—Fiction.   I. Title.
    PS3573.I5332S24 2010
    813'.54—dc22

                                     2010006718

Cover by Deborah Chabrian
Design by Marisa Jackson
Typeset by Aptara

Printed and bound in the United States of America

10 9 8 7 6 5 4 3 2 1

Acknowledgments

*I*n memory of the unforgettable Patricia Zimmerman, "Mrs. Z.," and in honor of Cookie Beck, Tara Oravec, Jill Morningstar, Terri Biesecker and Debi Duffey, who, despite their grief, put on happy faces to welcome the children of Trinity Nursery & Playschool. It was a privilege to work with you.

This story is for every huge-hearted person who left family, home and work to rescue animals left behind during Hurricane Katrina evacuation efforts. Saints do walk among us.

—Anne Marie Rodgers

GRACE CHAPEL INN

A place where one can be
refreshed and encouraged,
a place of hope and healing,
a place where God is at home.

Chapter One

"Good morning." Alice Howard entered the kitchen of Grace Chapel Inn with a smile. The kitchen was one of her favorite rooms, with its cheerful paprika-painted cabinets, black-and-white tiled floor and maple accents.

Her sister Jane already was working on breakfast, expertly cracking eggs into a bowl with one hand. Jane's long dark hair was twisted up at the back of her head, and she wore robin's-egg-blue cotton pants. An oversize shirt in the same hue covered a white knit T-shirt. When she spotted Alice, Jane stopped her baking preparations and wiped her hands. "Good morning."

Alice, Jane and their eldest sister Louise had inherited the imposing Victorian family home upon their father's passing. Since then, they had successfully transformed their treasured home into an inn.

Jane handed Alice a mug of hot tea from which a welcoming wisp of steam curled. "I can't wait for you to try this new blend. Time for Tea just received a new selection of British teas, and Wilhelm recommended this one especially for you."

Wilhelm Wood owned the small, elegant tea shop on Berry Lane in the small town of Acorn Hill, Pennsylvania.

"What's it called?" Alice cupped her hands around the warm mug with a grateful smile. Her bobbed coppery hair was brushed, and over her white uniform she was wearing a pink nurse's smock printed with bandaged teddy bears. She would leave soon for an upcoming shift at the hospital in Potterston.

"Bluebell Delight," Jane replied. "I bought several new flavors to try out on our guests, but I thought we should sample them first."

Alice inhaled the fragrant scents from the drink. "This smells wonderful." She walked to the small television that the sisters kept in a corner and picked up the remote control. "Isn't it silly to keep the remote control beside the TV?" she asked whimsically. "There's a reason it's called a remote, you know."

Jane laughed, her blue eyes twinkling. "I never thought about it. We watch it so seldom."

Alice nodded. People frequently remarked on the peace and tranquillity the inn afforded its guests, something the sisters attributed to the absence of televisions and computer access in the rooms. The small TV in the kitchen was the only one in the entire inn. It was used sparingly to watch the news or an occasional cooking show.

Alice turned on the television. "I'm anxious about how things are going down south today."

Jane's expression sobered. "Oh, those poor dear people. I can hardly imagine the suffering."

Five days earlier, a late-season hurricane had barreled into the Gulf Coast of the United States, devastating sections of Florida and Alabama. The images of dazed survivors wandering through rubble searching for family members had riveted the nation ever since. Relief efforts streaming into the region from around the country were experiencing frustrating delays because of the destruction. Roadways were blocked, and the Pensacola airport had been damaged so badly that it was closed to air traffic pending repairs.

The sounds of the news filled the kitchen as the network anchors shared more sad stories.

"Look, Jane." Alice stood before the television. "There's another dog. Isn't anyone doing anything for the animals?" Worry marked her tone. With her soft heart and gentle nature, Alice had a genuine affection for animals. As a child, she had been drawn to help creatures in distress, and she now watched the hurricane coverage anxiously as reporters focused on human stories while saying very little about the plight of companion animals and wildlife in the affected areas.

Jane came to stand beside her sister. On the news program, a small white dog cowered beneath a plank propped at a crooked angle against a concrete slab. The little dog took several tentative steps toward the woman with the microphone. "Animals are everywhere," the reporter said. "The weather bureau did not expect this to become a category four storm, and people who evacuated assumed they'd be coming home again in a day or so." She gestured to the pile of rubble and to the dog. "This dog is probably someone's pet, perhaps left at home with food and water."

As she finished her broadcast, she walked away from the white dog without a backward glance.

"What is wrong with her?" Alice demanded. "How could she just walk away from that poor little creature? He was looking to her for help." Alice was near tears.

Jane put a comforting arm around her older sister's shoulders. "Maybe after the cameras were turned off, they did help," she suggested.

"I hope so." But Alice didn't sound convinced. "I know it's important to focus on saving human lives, but I don't understand why animals can't be helped at the same time."

"Come sit down." Jane waved Alice toward the table. "I'm making mushroom-and-mozzarella omelets this morning, and yours is almost ready." A chef by profession, Jane put her skills to good use preparing breakfasts for the inn's guests as well as for the sisters.

Alice sat but wasn't diverted from the topic. "Last night, I read in the newspaper that any animal-relief efforts have to wait until rescuers are certain they've taken care of all the people first. How long will that take? That little dog could die before anyone is allowed in there to give him food or water."

Jane winced. "Is there a Red Cross for animals? Who organizes relief efforts for something like this?"

Alice shrugged. "I have no idea. I've never heard of any organized rescue group for animals in disasters." Her brows drew together in an unusually fierce expression. "But there should be something."

"Should be something for what?" Louise Smith, Alice and Jane's oldest sister, swept into the kitchen. She was dressed in a simple but elegant navy suit with an ivory blouse and her signature string of pearls. Her short, stylishly cut hair gleamed silver in the bright kitchen light.

"For animals," Alice told her. Then she paused. "You look lovely today. Not that you don't usually," she added hastily. "But you're dressed up a bit more than normal."

"I am attending a seminar at the Riverton Historical Society today," Louise informed her.

"Oh, that's right," Jane said. "The one about Henry Harbaugh."

Louise nodded. "And the influence of the German Reformed Church in Pennsylvania."

"Didn't he write 'Jesus, I Live to Thee'?" Alice asked. "That's such a beautiful hymn." Her voice wavered. "It was one of Father's favorites."

"We sang it at his funeral," Jane remembered. She quoted. "'To die in Thee is life to me / In my eternal home.' What inspirational words."

"Yes. I found it comforting," Alice said, "to be reminded that Father's life in heaven was beginning."

"Have some tea." Jane set a mug in front of Louise as she took a seat. "I got some new varieties from Time for Tea. You and Alice are my guinea pigs."

Louise, like Alice before her, took an appreciative sniff. "If it tastes as good as it smells, it's a winner," she proclaimed.

❧

Alice's day passed quickly. It was the beginning of November and right on schedule, flu and pneumonia were beginning to make their annual pilgrimages through the southeastern Pennsylvania population. However, as busy as she was, Alice was unable to forget about the animals suffering in Florida. It seemed every patient in every room she visited had his or her television turned to news of the disaster.

While she was giving Mrs. Guilfoyle's granddaughter discharge instructions for the diabetic older woman, the other patient in the room was watching a disaster update. In the background, Alice caught a glimpse of two Siamese kittens rummaging through a destroyed home.

Those kittens need help, Alice thought. And the amorphous idea that had been forming in her brain all week finally took solid form. "I'm going there," she said aloud.

"Can I come too? I need milk and bread," said the aging dementia patient.

Alice laughed. "Of course you can," she said cheerfully, patting the woman's hand gently. Then, when she left the room, her work there completed, she said to herself again, "I'm going, if I can just figure out how to help."

⌒

Later that day, Alice returned home from work and changed her clothes, then checked in two new arrivals while Jane buzzed around in the kitchen, preparing the evening meal.

Louise came home as Jane finished making the Waldorf salad. "I invited Aunt Ethel for dinner. Perhaps we should eat in the dining room," she announced. "She's got some new plan to raise money for Helping Hands, and she can hardly wait to share it with us." Helping Hands was Grace Chapel's local outreach ministry, designed to assist residents.

Jane grinned. "I guarantee you our names are beside several volunteer jobs already."

As Alice hung up the red dish towel she'd been using, she said, "It's for a good cause, so I don't mind."

"Oh, I'm sure I won't either," Jane assured her. "I just hope my tasks involve baking something." She turned to Louise. "Is Lloyd also joining us?"

Lloyd Tynan was a special friend of Ethel's, and he frequently joined them for dinner when Ethel came.

"I don't believe so," Louise replied. "Aunt Ethel said there is an auction in Potterston tonight that he wants to attend. Apparently, there are a number of those political buttons and memorabilia that he collects up for bid."

Just then, a distinctive "Yoo-hoo!" sounded in the front hallway.

"There's Aunt Ethel now," Alice said.

"Excellent timing. This is just about ready." Jane expertly lifted the stuffed chicken with herb sauce onto a serving plate and set it on the counter with several other dishes.

Ethel Buckley entered the kitchen just after Jane had disappeared into the storage room to get a suitable tray. "Hello, dear," she said to Alice.

"Hello," Alice replied. She took in the particularly vibrant shade of her aunt's red hair. "Did you have your hair colored today? It's looking especially pretty."

Clearly pleased, Ethel patted her brilliant coiffure. "You have a good eye, Alice. I did, indeed." She sniffed the air. "What's for dinner? It smells delicious."

"Jane made baked chicken," Louise said as she led the way into the dining room. "But you know Jane—it's not just any old baked chicken. My taste buds are begging already."

Alice set new potatoes and snow peas on the table and began filling bowls with the Waldorf salad. Louise poured water into each of the pretty painted glasses that complemented the china.

Jane bustled into the dining room with a crowded tray that she set on the buffet. "Hi, Aunt Ethel." She stopped and took a closer look at her aunt. "Your hair looks…bright tonight. In a beautiful way, of course," she added.

Louise was smiling. "Titian Dreams, right? The name of the shade is quite fitting."

"I think so too." Ethel beamed. "Every time I glance in the mirror, I'm delighted."

As they all took their seats, Jane asked, "Alice, would you like to offer the prayer?"

The four women joined hands and Alice shared a prayer. She made special mention of the victims of the hurricane, including the animals that so concerned her. As they began to pass the dishes around the table, she said, "I came to a decision today."

"A decision about what?" Louise asked.

Alice took a deep breath. "About traveling down to help with animal rescue in the disaster area. I've been thinking about it for days, and I'm going to find out if there is a group I could volunteer to work with."

"Animal rescue?" Ethel looked puzzled. "Is there such a thing? I'd have thought you'd want to help some of those poor people."

"I do feel bad for the people. But there are hordes of relief workers heading down there to help the human victims. No one seems to care what happens to the animals. I keep seeing pictures on the news, and someone's got to do something!"

"Maybe," said Jane, "but I'm not sure it should be you, Alice. It could be dangerous down there."

Jane's comment unsettled Alice. She had counted on Jane to see her point of view.

"Yes," said Louise. "I agree with Jane. You could get into real trouble. They've deployed the National Guard to try to help keep order. I've heard there's looting going on and who knows what else."

"It's out of the question." Ethel set down her fork, a horrified expression on her face. "It's much too dangerous, dear. I just read in today's paper that they're worried about outbreaks of some very nasty diseases because of the unsanitary conditions."

Alice continued eating. She said a silent prayer for patience. "That's all the more reason for trained medical personnel to volunteer."

"Yes, but you're talking about helping animals," Louise pointed out. "What do you know about animal medicine?"

"Not very much," Alice admitted. "But there must be jobs I could help with. Not everything requires special training, you know. I imagine it's very similar to the hospital in some ways."

"Yuck!" said Jane. "You know what kind of jobs those will be."

"Probably better than any of you do." Alice was immediately sorry for the sharp edge to her tone. She took a deep breath and made an effort to speak calmly. "I can't just sit here and watch suffering occur, whether it's human or animal. I believe my skills could be useful there."

"Where would you go?" Louise asked. "I mean, specifically where? You can't just drive down to the area. There are roadblocks up around a significant amount of the disaster zone." She sat back and crossed her arms. "This is really not a good idea, Alice."

"No, it isn't," Ethel reiterated. "It's just too dangerous."

There was a moment of charged silence around the table. Alice did not trust herself to speak without anger and she kept her eyes on her plate as she battled an uncharacteristic urge to speak harshly. Was she the only person who believed that animals should receive the care and consideration that humans should?

Ethel meant well, Alice reminded herself. Her seemingly harsh comments had been made out of concern, as had Louise's. And her family had raised some good points. She needed to find out more about what efforts were underway, seek locations where she could go to help and find out if civilian aid would be permitted. Finding information on the Internet was a bit daunting to Alice, but maybe Jane would help later.

Jane cleared her throat. "Ultimately, the decision is Alice's," she reminded Louise and Ethel. "We have voiced our concerns and Alice has heard them. Why don't we change the topic?" As everyone began to eat again, she turned to Ethel. "Louise mentioned you had an idea to raise funds for the Helping Hands ministry. Why don't you tell us about it?"

Ethel's eyes lit up. "Well, as you may know, we depend entirely on donations. And frankly, we haven't received the support we had hoped for this year. So I started thinking about ways to raise money and decided we should have a crafts fair."

"A crafts fair?" Louise looked doubtful. "You mean you would have people selling things during the social hour and after church?"

"No, no." Ethel shook her head. "I mean a real crafts fair. One that could be held—and improved on—annually. The high school band supporters hold a crafts fair every spring to benefit the band. I got to thinking that a similar activity might be a good project for us. Theirs always gathers quite a crowd. I think there would be enough interest in the community to hold one in the autumn."

"Where would you have it?" Jane asked.

"In the Assembly Room at the chapel. I've already pitched the idea to the Seniors Social Circle and they liked it although they got a bit overwhelmed thinking about how to implement it."

"So you would chair it?" Alice asked. Heaven knew Ethel could organize a litter of kittens to walk in a straight line. However, she never would be listed on a Top Ten Tactful People list, and the potential for problems was a concern.

Ethel nodded.

"When would you have the first one?"

"Sometime next fall. I was thinking October, around the harvest season."

Louise shook her head. "Everyone and his brother have craft shows while the weather is mild in September and October. Hold it the first Saturday in December, and market it as an opportunity to pick up hand-made gifts and Christmas goodies. That's sure to be successful."

Ethel sat up straighter. "That's a wonderful idea. If we do that, we could have one this year!"

There was another silence around the table as the three younger women realized they really had heard their aunt correctly.

Jane's eyes were wide as she asked, "Don't you think that's a bit…ambitious, Aunt Ethel? The first week in December is only a month away!"

"Yes," said Louise. "I really don't think—"

"Oh, nonsense," said Ethel in a robust tone. "So we'll start small and expand it next year."

"If it's successful," Alice qualified.

"Of course it'll be successful." In Ethel's mind, that was a given. By now she was practically rubbing her hands together. "We'll sell places for booths to local crafters, and the Grace Chapel congregation will also make craft items. We can profit even more if we run a concession area for lunch and have a selection of baked goods for sale."

"Goodness, that sounds like a lot of planning," Alice said faintly. "I suppose if you're going to try all those things, you might want to have each crafter donate one item for a raffle or a silent auction."

"I think that a silent auction requires too many volunteers," Louise put in. "You need a lot of people to oversee the bidding, or you wind up with unhappy bidders who are sure someone else did something wrong."

"That's true, unfortunately," Jane said.

"But you could let people purchase tickets," Louise continued. "Place a box in front of each raffle item, and people could pop their tickets into the box for the item they want to win. They could put one ticket in several different boxes or fill one box with a bunch of tickets if there is something they want badly. Then at the end of the fair, a winning ticket is drawn from each box."

"Would people have to be there to win?" Jane asked. "That could be a hassle."

"No." Louise shook her head. "We could ask them to write their names and phone numbers on each ticket. After the crafts fair is over, we could deliver the winning items or hold them at the church office and let the winners come pick them up."

"Oh, you girls have been an enormous help," Ethel cried. "And you have such wonderful ideas. You all should be on the crafts-making committee."

"I don't believe I'll have time." Louise barely missed a beat. "I recently picked up two new piano students, and I had hoped to visit Cynthia in Boston before Thanksgiving as well."

She barely had the words out before Alice said, "I'm sorry, but I can't commit to that if I'm not even going to be in town. I probably will be able to help by the day of the event though."

"I can do that too," said Louise.

"Well," said Ethel with a heavy sigh. "I suppose that leaves you and me to plan this, Jane."

"I—"

"Why don't you chair the crafts committee? If you're able to take care of that, I'll deal with the setup and the food and the raffle and all those types of details."

"I suppose I could do that," Jane said faintly.

As the one who was often on the receiving end of her aunt's well-meant orders, Alice could not help but be grateful that she had had a legitimate reason to decline.

"You'll need to find people to serve on your committee."

"My committee?"

"And since you're going to be talking with people about crafts, why don't you check around and see who might be interested in purchasing space for a booth?"

"Why don't I?" Jane shrugged her shoulders in resignation. "And while I'm at it, I might as well volunteer to make a few items for the baked-goods table."

"Oh, good," said Ethel. "You could—"

"And if this idea flies," Jane said, "why don't you contact Zack and Nancy Colwin to see if they'd chair the baked-goods committee?"

"That's a good idea." Ethel looked around, instantly diverted. "I need a pencil and paper to jot down all these ideas."

As Alice rose to find the requested items, Louise cautioned her aunt, "Don't forget that a project of this scope will require a vote of the church board."

"Yes," said Alice. "I hope you won't be too disappointed if people don't feel they are up to rushing this into production in such a short time."

"Does that mean you plan to vote against it?" Ethel immediately looked suspicious.

"No, I think it's an exciting idea," said Alice.

"Particularly since you aren't getting stuck with the work," muttered Jane in an undertone as she rose to retrieve the dessert she'd brought in earlier.

Alice smiled at her sister. "Exactly," she agreed with a laugh.

"But seriously, Aunt Ethel," said Louise. "This is a big undertaking even if you only do half of the things we just discussed, and Alice is right—there is not much time to plan."

Ethel lifted her chin. "If the good Lord is involved, we can't fail."

Jane met Alice's glance, and the sisters smiled.

"I suspect you'll have no trouble persuading folks to your way of thinking," Jane predicted.

Chapter Two

*J*ane went down to the Clip 'n' Curl the following Monday morning to get the ends of her long dark hair trimmed, as she did every six months or so. Betty Dunkle, the owner of the shop, always tried to talk Jane into a cut and perm, telling her a shorter style would make her look younger, but so far Jane had resisted. She liked her hair just the way it was and found it especially easy to twist up out of the way when she was cooking.

She was sitting in one of the cracked leather chairs in the waiting area when a headline from the Philadelphia newspaper, which had been tossed in a nearby basket, caught her eye. VOLUNTEERS AID IN ANIMAL-RESCUE EFFORTS, read the headline. And in smaller type below that, CARE AND COMFORT FOR SUFFERING PETS.

Perhaps this would interest Alice. Picking up the article, Jane skimmed the content.

"Would you mind if I took this home?" she asked Betty when the hairdresser called her name.

"Go right ahead. I read it yesterday," Betty told her. She held up a lock of Jane's hair and swished it back and forth. "Are you going to let me take a few inches off this and layer it?"

"No!" Jane put a hand protectively to her head. "Just a trim, please."

"You said you'd think about it." Betty sighed dramatically as she began to section and pin Jane's hair out of the way.

"And I have," Jane assured her. "I just haven't *finished* thinking about it."

Betty smiled, knowing when she had lost a skirmish. "Okay. Just keep it in mind."

Jane headed home immediately after her hair appointment, the newspaper beside her on the seat of her car.

As she turned into the gravel driveway to the left of the graceful old Victorian, she spotted Alice sweeping the large porch. Braking, she rolled down her window and called, "Alice, I have something for you." She grabbed the newspaper and waved it out the window.

Alice's brown eyes lit up with curiosity. She leaned the broom against the doorframe, grabbed the old flannel shirt she had worn over her T-shirt until she became too warm and hurried off the porch. "What is it?" She took the newspaper Jane offered.

"Read the lead article," Jane said. "It's about animal-rescue efforts in the disaster area. I thought of you right away."

"Oh, thank you!" Alice clutched the newspaper, completely forgetting the broom, and hurried indoors as Jane continued on to the parking lot at the back corner of the inn. Her sister's excitement reminded Jane to try to be more supportive of Alice's interest in a trip down south to help the animals. She had felt bad on Saturday evening when they all inadvertently trampled on Alice's enthusiasm with their concerns for her safety. She was sure Alice understood that their criticism, candidly expressed as they had been, were rooted in loving concern. But she also knew from personal experience on the receiving end of Ethel's "suggestions" that they could sting.

Entering the kitchen, she found that Alice had spread out the paper on the kitchen table and was eagerly scanning the article. Wendell, the family's gray tabby cat, lounged in a patch of sun coming through the window, but he rose to his feet as he saw Jane enter the room.

"Look at this, Jane," her sister said. She pointed at a line in the article. "This woman—Shelby Riverly—was interviewed about her experiences at an animal-rescue camp. She says volunteers are desperately needed and probably will be for quite some time."

Jane nodded. She bent to run a hand over the soft fur of the cat's back, smiling as he arched and butted her palm with his head for a second pat. "I read the article. I thought perhaps you could contact her to get more information about how to organize a trip."

"Oh, thank you." Alice rose and hugged her sister. "I truly feel a calling to do this. But after listening to all of you Saturday evening, I started to think maybe I was foolish to even consider it."

Jane shook her head. "We're just concerned for you, and we didn't express ourselves particularly well. If you want to go, Alice, I'll do whatever I can to help."

Alice smiled. "You're going to have your hands full with that committee for Aunt Ethel's crafts fair. But just knowing you don't think I'm crazy is helpful. Oh! I almost forgot." She held up her hand. "Fred Humbert called. Aunt Ethel got the Seniors Social Circle together after church yesterday, and they decided to ask the board for permission to use the Assembly Room for a small-scale crafts fair. If Fred can gather enough members, there will be a special meeting of the board tonight to vote on it."

"Small scale?" Jane chuckled. "I don't believe our aunt knows the meaning of that phrase."

Alice nodded. "She is quite...enthusiastic about this idea."

"I don't know whether to hope they approve it or think Aunt Ethel's wacky for trying to put it together in such a short time," Jane said. She glanced at her watch. "Yikes! I've got work to do in the kitchen. Don't forget you left the broom on the front porch."

Alice entered the Grace Chapel Assembly Room shortly before seven that evening for the emergency board meeting. To her surprise, nearly every board member already had arrived. Lloyd Tynan and Ethel waved at her from their side-by-side seats across the table, as did both Pastor Ley and Rev. Kenneth Thompson. Patsy Ley, who like Pastor Thompson was not a board member, sat in her usual spot preparing to take minutes, and Fred Humbert smiled at Alice from his place at the end of the table, where he presided over the meetings.

"Hello, Alice. You're the last person we're waiting for because June Carter can't make it tonight." He cleared his throat and announced. "I'd like to call this special meeting of the Grace Chapel Board of Directors to order."

Fred swiftly dispensed with the essentials of *Robert's Rules of Order*, and then Lloyd made a motion to open a discussion of the proposed crafts fair.

"I second," announced Florence Simpson. Her broad forehead was furrowed, and her carefully applied lipstick emphasized the scowl that turned down the corners of her lips. "Now what, exactly, is this all about, Ethel?"

Alice knew that Florence hosted a small Christmas crafts get-together each December, and she considered herself quite creative. Although it had not occurred to Alice until now, she suspected that Florence's nose might be out of joint for not being included in the planning of this project.

Ethel rose majestically from her chair and proceeded to pass around a handout in outline form to each member of the board. As she explained the Seniors Social Circle's idea, her niece glanced around the room, trying to gauge each board member's opinion.

Sylvia Songer and Lloyd were openly smiling and nodding, while Cyril Overstreet and Fred listened attentively. Henry Ley also was smiling, as was the senior pastor, Rev. Thompson, who attended as an observer. Alice's glance moved past him to Florence. The woman's penciled eyebrows now had merged into one forbidding line.

The moment Ethel stopped speaking, Florence responded. "I think it would be a huge mistake to rush into something like this," she said firmly. "Good-quality crafts take time to prepare, and a craft show requires more planning than you could possibly manage in one month."

"If you'll take a minute to look over your handout, you'll see that I have planned the details quite carefully and I believe it is very possible." Ethel's voice dripped with so much patience that her annoyance could not be doubted. She and Florence were good friends—most of the time—but Alice knew the two prickly personalities could irritate each other at times.

Fred cleared his throat, waving his handout. "This does look like a lot of work to do in a short time, Ethel. Are you sure you could pull this off?"

"Oh yes," Aunt Ethel said. "I already have volunteers lined up to chair the committees for the crafts, the concessions, the baked goods and the setup. In fact, my niece Jane has agreed to chair the crafts committee. You all know that Jane is energetic and diplomatic, and I think she will do a marvelous job of finding vendors to fill our booths."

Alice couldn't help smiling. Ethel failed to mention that most of her volunteers, including Jane, had been conscripted.

"But does Jane know enough about crafts?" Florence asked.

Ethel drew in a deep breath, and Alice could see her feathers were ruffled. "Jane is excellent at a variety of crafts. She's a first-rate organizer, and she's *very good with people.*" Ethel emphasized the last four words.

"I'm not talking about simply asking people to participate," Florence huffed. "Most craft sellers work for months to prepare for a show. I can't imagine you're going to have many of them interested in purchasing booth space."

"Then it will be a very small first effort," Ethel said. "But I don't see the point of waiting until next year to get started. Even a modest crafts fair this year would acquaint people with our event, and next year could be much bigger."

The board continued to question Ethel about the details of the plan. Alice's aunt had an answer for every question, but she clearly was a bit affronted at their lack of confidence.

Ethel was receiving much the same treatment as she had doled out to Alice on Saturday evening. Although she had been annoyed with Ethel at the time, she felt a strong need to defend her aunt now. Alice was just about to affirm her confidence in her aunt's ability to pull off the crafts fair when Sylvia spoke up.

"I think it's a marvelous idea," Sylvia said. "If Jane would be interested, I'd be happy to serve on her committee."

"There is no committee until we vote," Florence said. "And in any case, is Ethel the best qualified for this job? It seems to me that someone who is already interested in and involved in local crafts might be a better choice."

No one spoke. Alice watched, fascinated, as Ethel's face turned an interesting shade of purple that clashed terribly with her hair. "Someone who cares enough to come up with a fund-raising idea certainly would be a better choice than someone who has seldom bothered to get involved with the Helping Hands ministry," Ethel said in a pointed tone.

"Why don't we move on to a vote if everyone has considered the issue?" Fred suggested. He looked apprehensive. Alice could not blame him. Anyone with any sense would dive for cover when Ethel and Florence were ready for combat.

Lloyd cleared his throat. "I move that the board appoint Ethel Buckley to chair the first Grace Chapel Crafts Fair to benefit the Helping Hands ministry."

"I second," Sylvia added enthusiastically.

"It has been moved and seconded that we appoint Ethel Buckley to chair the first Grace Chapel Crafts Fair to benefit the Helping Hands ministry," Fred pronounced. "All those in favor, please signify by raising your hands. Ethel, you'll abstain, of course, since this motion directly involves you."

Alice immediately raised her hand, as did Lloyd, Pastor Ley and Sylvia. Cyril followed suit a moment later. Then Fred asked for those opposed, and no one appeared surprised when Florence's hand shot into the air.

"I also vote in favor," Fred said. "So the final vote is six in favor, one opposed, one abstention and one absence. Ethel, we would like you to report on your progress at the regular monthly meeting."

Ethel smiled, obviously pleased that she had managed to persuade most of the board to support her. "Gladly. Thank you so much. This is going to be the start of something wonderful."

"Meeting adjourned!" Fred banged his gavel with a broad smile.

Florence's face was set as she rose and grabbed the cashmere jacket she had draped over the back of her chair. Muttering something about, ". . . don't have the sense to listen to the voice of reason," she stomped out of the room.

⌒

The next morning, Alice had just finished breakfast with Jane when Louise came into the kitchen. "How did it go last night?" she asked Alice.

"Aunt Ethel's idea got the board's support," Alice reported. "Although she and Florence probably aren't going to be on speaking terms for a while." She went on to tell them the details of the discussion and Florence's unforgettable exit.

Louise's eyebrows rose. "So Florence isn't going to be much help, I suppose?"

"I don't know about that," Jane said reflectively. "It seems to me that she might come around if she were asked to help with a special project or something."

"That's a good idea," Alice agreed. "I know she can be a trial, but Florence needs to feel included. Now that the vote is over, I think we all should try to make her feel she can make some important contributions to the crafts fair."

"You're right, Alice," said Jane. "But it sounds to me as if that will require a direct invitation from Aunt Ethel in there somewhere."

"Why don't you give it a shot first?" Louise suggested. "I'm not so sure Ethel and Florence will be ready to talk just yet. This way, if Florence doesn't react graciously, Aunt Ethel doesn't even need to know we asked."

Jane nodded. "Good point. Okay. I'll try to sweet-talk Florence."

The sisters shared wry smiles.

"I was thinking that the ANGELs could become involved with a craft," Alice said, referring to the church group of middle-school-aged girls she had founded and with whom she still met each week. "We have been learning about macramé, and I believe the girls could make some pretty bracelets with embroidery floss."

"Thank you, Alice. I think those will make lovely Christmas gifts."

"You should make a sign to advertise them," Louise said.

"Maybe you could do that for me," Alice said to her elder sister.

Louise opened her mouth, then closed it again and smiled. "I suppose I asked for that job, didn't I?"

Jane nodded, chuckling. "Just like I 'volunteered' to head up the crafts committee."

"It won't be so bad," Alice said. "Just don't forget to talk with Sylvia. She'll be a great resource."

"Don't worry," Jane assured her fervently. "Sylvia's shop is going to be my very first visit tomorrow morning!"

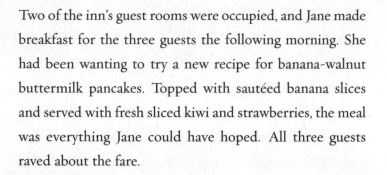

Two of the inn's guest rooms were occupied, and Jane made breakfast for the three guests the following morning. She had been wanting to try a new recipe for banana-walnut buttermilk pancakes. Topped with sautéed banana slices and served with fresh sliced kiwi and strawberries, the meal was everything Jane could have hoped. All three guests raved about the fare.

The single gentleman, Silas Cornish, was on a trip north to visit one of his children. He checked out and went on his way shortly after eating. The couple in the Sunrise Room, the Dickersons, was from Georgia. Civil War buffs, they had planned a day trip to the Gettysburg Battlefield approximately two hours away, and after receiving directions from Jane, they set off as well.

As soon as the breakfast dishes were cleaned up, Jane donned a lightweight jacket and walked into Acorn Hill, the small town she had called home as a child. Returning to live here after her father died had been the smartest decision of her life. She still felt a twinge of regret that she had not been here more while he was living.

She gave a contented sigh as she moved along Hill Street at a leisurely pace. Walking the town's lovely brick sidewalks and waving at the many familiar faces still gave her a warm glow. She had lived away from the area for years until she and her sisters opened the inn. Coming home, to Jane, had meant far more than simply returning to the home of her youth. It meant comfort and familiarity, friendship and acceptance.

As she walked along the tree-lined streets, Jane enjoyed the unseasonably mild weather. November was often chilly or downright cold, with possibilities of early snows. However, this November had been utterly lovely, with temperatures so mild she actually raked leaves in a short-sleeved shirt the other day.

Sylvia's Buttons was on Acorn Avenue, just around the corner from the Good Apple Bakery. The little sewing shop occupied the ground floor of a two-story building made of warm, rosy-pink brick.

Jane paused for a moment to admire the window dressing before entering the shop. Sylvia always had such creative ideas. The current window display featured a stunning variety of quilts that Sylvia took on consignment for women in the Amish community around Lancaster. Sylvia had chosen quilts with predominantly autumn colors, and the background of the window was ablaze in crimsons, rusts, brilliant golds and oranges, soft browns and even a few muted greens.

Scattered along the bottom of the display were soft sculptured pillows in the shape of leaves: long, slender oak leaves, three-pointed maple leaves, and an elongated oval that might represent elm or black walnut. Sylvia even had made some adorable acorn pillows, which were scattered among the leaves.

Jane pushed through the door, setting the bell attached to it jingling. "Good morning."

"Good morning, Jane." Sylvia was an attractive forty-something with strawberry blonde hair. Today it was twisted up in a messy bun that was charming in a distinctly Sylvia kind of way. She wore a simple denim dress with more than a dozen safety pins fastened through one of the pockets, and two needles threaded with white were stuck through the other. Around one wrist was a stuffed fabric heart attached to an elastic band, and it bristled with a forest of straight pins.

Sylvia's shop was a kaleidoscope of color. Quilt fabric covered one long wall, bolt after bolt of small prints and solids in every color imaginable. A selection of other fabrics suitable for garments made a maze of the interior floor space. Sewing notions, threads, other needlework accessories and craft kits were on display as well.

In the middle of the shop was a large table for cutting patterns and laying out projects. As Jane approached, Sylvia straightened from the quilt she had been working on, massaging her lower back with both hands. "I bet I can guess why you're here."

Jane grinned. "I bet you can. I'm sure my aunt Ethel asked you for your input on this crafts fair."

"Actually, I volunteered." Sylvia smiled back. "I think it's a wonderful idea, and I'll be more than happy to help."

"Oh, good. You'll be my very first committee member." Jane pulled a notebook from the capacious bag she had slung over one shoulder. "The next thing I'd like to do is pick your brain for the names of crafters who might be interested in participating."

"Do we have to call them?" Sylvia sounded apprehensive, and Jane remembered that although Sylvia was a successful business owner, deep down she was rather shy.

"No, I told Aunt Ethel I would generate a list, and she promised to find me some other volunteers to begin inviting them." Jane rolled her eyes. "We're going to be quite busy as it is, organizing craft ideas for the congregation to work on."

"All right." Sylvia began listing the names of local crafters whom Ethel could contact, while Jane dutifully scribbled down every name. When they finished, Jane put aside the list to give to her aunt.

"Now we need some ideas for crafts our church members and friends can help to make," Jane said.

"Why don't we start with the people we know we can count on to make their specialties," Sylvia suggested. "Several members of my intermediate crochet class might help. One lady makes those cotton dishcloths that everyone loves, and I bet we could get someone to donate a baby layette for the raffle."

"That's a wonderful idea." Jane started a new list. "I also have a suggestion: Louise has a piano student whose mother always brings cross-stitch to work on while she waits for him. The child's name is Bobby something-or-other—"

"Oh, you mean Bobby Pfiffer. His mother's name is Monique. She comes in here for DMC floss all the time."

"Yes, that's it. The last time she was at the house, she was cross-stitching Christmas ornaments. I thought perhaps we could ask her to lead a group of cross-stitchers to make some simple ornaments."

Sylvia rushed over to a rack of craft items. "Here!" She waved a package at Jane. "These are little, gold plastic heart frames. Helpers could cross-stitch simple designs and frame them with these."

"That's a great idea!"

"And oh! Here's another thought—I could design a simple cross-stitch pattern of Grace Chapel. I bet they would sell like hotcakes."

Jane was writing madly. "I'm sure they would. What else could we do?"

"Mabel Torrence makes gorgeous knitted scarves. You know the ones everyone is wearing these days, with feathery and metallic threads, and super-soft luxury yarns? I'm sure there are other members of the Seniors Social Circle who knit. Perhaps Mabel would organize a group of them to make scarves."

"I'd buy one," Jane declared as she wrote down that idea. "I think they're beautiful."

"I also have a pattern for a microwave bag that bakes potatoes just like the oven does."

"Really? How does it work?" Jane was instantly intrigued. While she had a thousand uses for the microwave oven, she generally used it to aid in her preparations and rarely relied on it for the finished product. There was just no substitute for an oven-baked meal.

"I have no idea. I saw one being demonstrated at a craft show last summer. The potato tasted exactly as if it had been baked, so I bought one of the bags and took it apart. I was sure there had to be some special lining, but it's just a fabric bag. I could write up the directions and find a few volunteers to make them."

"I'm sure some of the seniors would help." Jane made herself a note to mention it to them.

"And note cards would be another easy craft idea."

"Note cards?" Jane envisioned stick-figure sketches.

"Like these." Sylvia lofted a package toward Jane.

Catching it in midair, Jane opened the sealed plastic sandwich bag and pulled out eight simple note cards. Made of a finely woven heavyweight paper, there were two each of four designs glued onto the front. The first was a simple Christmas tree cut out of printed green scrap fabric. The edges were sealed with a product designed to prevent fraying, and the print on the fabric gave the impression of ornaments. The tree was topped with a simple star of some shiny gold fabric.

The second was a set of two flat fabric bells, one glued to overlap the other a bit. A red bow garnished the top, and it looked as though the bells were ringing. Yet another note card design was a wreath made of felt holly leaves and tiny red circles for berries with a ribbon bow. The final one was a Christmas gift in a deep red print with shiny silver ribbon "wrapping" it, and a silver bow glued at the top.

"I taught a 4-H club in Potterston how to make these for a fund-raiser," Sylvia explained. "I would be happy to help a group of volunteers make some to sell at the crafts fair."

"I'm getting excited about this," Jane declared. "We're going to have some lovely things to offer. Already we have more than I'd expected to come up with."

"I was thinking," Sylvia said tentatively, "that perhaps we could ask Florence to contribute. She wasn't very happy last night at the meeting, and I thought that if she felt needed, she might be more supportive."

"I agree." Jane thought of her conversation with Alice and Louise just a few hours ago. "I'm going to speak with her this afternoon. Any good ideas on how to present this?"

"Very carefully," Sylvia said with a sly smile.

Jane laughed. "Exactly."

Chapter Three

As soon as she returned home from her planning session with Sylvia, Jane called Florence to make arrangements for a visit.

"What's this about?" Florence asked suspiciously.

"My aunt has asked me to chair the crafts committee for the upcoming crafts fair." Jane strove for an innocent tone. "You immediately sprang to mind since you're the local expert on crafts. If you're interested, I would like to talk with you about some ideas I have had. I know you're a busy person, though, so I will understand if you can't fit me in."

There was a short silence. "All right," Florence finally said. "You can visit around two o'clock today and tell me what you're planning."

It was a good thing she had not made any plans for the afternoon, Jane thought a short while later as she parked her car in front of the Simpsons' lovely brick home.

Florence had not even appeared to consider that Jane might not be able to see her that very day.

She knocked on the beautiful mahogany door, eyeing the colorful autumn arrangement displayed there. Florence's tastes, like Jane's sister Louise's, veered toward what Jane considered a formal, traditional look. Jane herself preferred simple, clean, uncluttered modern lines.

Florence answered the door so quickly that Jane supposed she had been peeking out a window waiting for her guest. "Come in, Jane," she said graciously.

Florence was a heavy woman. She dressed carefully and usually looked well put together. Today she was wearing brown slacks with an oatmeal-colored cotton sweater covered with embroidered squirrels and acorns. Gold acorns hung from a chunky necklace of deep green, sand, rust and brown polished stones separated by small gold beads, and similar acorns hung from her ears. Florence was quite possibly the only person Jane knew who could afford to buy jewelry to match one specific outfit. Though to be fair, the pieces could be worn with any autumn-colored clothing.

Florence hung Jane's coat in a hall closet and led the way into her formal living room. The room was crowded with antiques, large pieces of leather and mahogany furniture. Brocade curtains tied back with gold rope swept to the floor and added to the cluttered look. Several large oil paintings in ornate gilded frames hung on the walls, while pieces of ornamental china, silver and crystal covered nearly every surface. Two mahogany display cabinets held additional expensive dishes and knickknacks that Jane knew were pieces passed down through several generations of her family. Jane wondered how Ronald, Florence's husband, felt about living in a museum dedicated to Florence's family history.

"Sit down, Jane." Florence indicated a wingback chair as she settled herself on a loveseat nearby. "Would you like some tea?"

"That would be lovely." Jane was amused to note that Florence actually had a silver tea set on the table before them. It held a small selection of petit fours, delicate china plates and cups, and a dish of mixed nuts. She took a cup and saucer from Florence, hiding a smile. Florence was keen on appearances; she loved to play lady of the manor. Jane could not see the harm in letting Florence enjoy the moment even though it would cut into Jane's afternoon more than she had hoped.

As she suffered through tea and small talk, she struggled to hide her impatience. She consoled herself with the reassurance that Florence would be in a more receptive frame of mind if Jane indulged her for a while.

Finally, *finally*, Florence delicately patted her lips with the linen napkin she had been using and set it aside. "So tell me about this wild idea," she said. "I understand you're in charge of crafts?"

And just like that, Jane understood the real problem. Florence's feelings were hurt. Beneath the belligerent tone Florence had used was a tiny, telltale quaver.

"I am," Jane said, "but all I'm going to be doing is organizing the crafts that will be offered for sale. You know my talents are far more suited to cooking. I really need skilled craftspeople to volunteer a little of their time as well."

"I'm sure it's going to fail. Ethel doesn't begin to have adequate time to plan such a big undertaking."

"I believe they are intending to start small." It was not a lie, although Jane was pretty sure her aunt had bigger plans in mind. "If you're not interested in participating, we can try to find someone else. But you know, Florence, there is probably no one else in the community who could come up with such original and lovely creations as yours." She was quite sincere, even though she had an ulterior motive for the compliment. She had seen some of Florence's crafts and flower arrangements. While they were not always to her more contemporary tastes, Florence definitely had an eye for color and design.

Florence almost visibly swelled with pride. "Thank you, Jane. I like to think I have a gift."

"You do, indeed."

"Perhaps there is something I could do."

"I'm certainly open to any ideas. To be honest, I was hoping I could talk you into getting your craft group together to make several different items. Alice mentioned that you have a get-together every year around Christmas."

Florence frowned. "I don't know how many things we really can get done in such a short time frame." She was determined to hammer away at that theme.

"I'd be grateful for even one idea," Jane told her. Then she added, "I spoke with Sylvia this morning and she came up with several." True, Sylvia was not actually making all of them, but the note cards, microwave bags and Grace Chapel cross-stitch ornaments all were her ideas, and she also was the one to suggest the knitting projects.

"Well, of course I could come up with several if I choose."

"I'm sure you could. And I'm equally sure each would be a big hit. Aunt Ethel has one of those little sleighs made of a woven basket that you crafted several years ago. I've always thought it was lovely. She displays it every Christmas." Jane felt it might not hurt to remind Florence that Ethel did value her friendship.

"Oh, those old things. They take barely any time at all."

"By the way, how did you make the runners curve like that?" Jane was genuinely curious.

"I soak thin strips of grapevine in water so that they're pliable," Florence told her. "Very, very easy. In fact, I know my craft club and I could have more than a dozen of those ready for you."

"Oh, Florence, that would be wonderful! The finished product is so impressive."

"Speaking of grapevine, I have a number of miniature wreaths laid away that I could donate. I dried apples and mums to add to them. I think they're going to be lovely."

Jane got out her notebook. "Thank you so much! May I put you down for the grapevine wreaths and the basket sleighs?"

"Of course. And how about hand-painted welcome signs? I have a beautiful design that I made several years ago that a number of people have asked me about. Several of my friends are good folk-art painters, and I know those would sell quickly." With that, Florence was off and running so fast that Jane had a hard time writing down everything she was saying.

By the time Florence finished, Jane had a list of seven craft items that Florence was sure she and her friends could contribute.

"Are you sure you want to commit to all of these? It seems like an awful lot to ask of you." Jane looked over her notes with concern. Perhaps she had been a little too encouraging.

"Nonsense! It'll be no trouble at all. And are you going to need people to work at the church's booths?"

"Most definitely, and at the raffle and the food concession. Sylvia has volunteered, and Alice, Louise and I plan to help. But we could use more."

"Let me check with some of my friends in the congregation. I'm certain some of them would be happy to help us."

Jane was delighted at Florence's use of the inclusive pronoun. It certainly seemed as if the mission to smooth Florence's feathers had been successful. Still, Jane made a mental note to appeal to Ethel to deal gently with Florence.

Goodness! That was probably going to take as much finesse as today's visit had. *Lord*, Jane said silently, *give me the patience to handle these strong-willed ladies with kindness and understanding.* She smiled to herself. *Especially since it's possible that I'll be just like them some day.*

૭

When the slight, blonde woman with the toddler in tow came through the door of the inn Saturday afternoon, Alice was puzzled. They did not have a reservation for anyone with children.

She smiled kindly at the woman as she paused on the rug in front of the reception desk. "Welcome to Grace Chapel Inn. May I help you?"

"I'm looking for Alice Howard."

"I'm Alice." Sudden comprehension dawned. "You must be Shelby."

The younger woman smiled and extended a hand. "Yes, and this is Jonathan. Hello, Alice. It's nice to meet you."

"Oh, you too! Hello, Jonathan." Alice shook Shelby's hand and chuckled when the child clutched at his mother's leg. Then she came around the desk and ushered her guests toward the living room across from the gleaming mahogany balustrade of the staircase. "I have so many questions about your trip down to the disaster area."

"I'm glad you called," said Shelby as she took the seat Alice indicated on the overstuffed burgundy sofa. Jonathan sat down beside her. "I would love to go back, but I simply can't leave my family for an extended period again. I'm compromising by talking about it to any poor soul who will listen to me, and by trying to recruit others to go." She smiled down at the little boy who clung to her. "It was hard to be away for two weeks."

"That's a long time." Alice took a seat in the matching chair and smiled at Jonathan. "I bet you're glad your mommy is home again."

The little boy shot her a shy smile before turning his face into Shelby's side.

"I didn't intend to be gone more than a week." Shelby shook her head. "But once you get down there, it's hard to leave. You realize how desperately every pair of hands is needed."

Alice sat forward. "Where did you go? And how did you find out about it? I want to help, but I'd like to make sure I will be needed wherever I go."

"Oh, you'll be needed. But you might not be able to talk to anyone ahead of time because there's no phone or electric service for miles around."

"But surely by now they've got some service. It's been almost three weeks."

Shelby shook her head. "Until you get down there, you can't imagine the scale of devastation. It's going to be months before most utilities are anywhere close to normal service again." She dug into the large denim shoulder bag she had set on the floor by her chair. "I have a fact sheet here. The camp we went to is called Camp Compassion. It's almost a dozen miles outside the worst part of the disaster area, which could be dangerous for strangers, especially after dark."

"How did you ever find it?"

"After the hurricane, I got online to see if any of the big animal-rescue groups were organizing efforts and found that one of them had set up a bulletin board for volunteers. People returning from the area posted notes about their experiences, and people wanting to go posted questions and requests for traveling companions in their region."

"Did you go alone?"

Shelby shook her head. "No. I have a friend from my church who is a dog lover, and I approached her about going. When I did, she said she had been thinking the exact same thing. So we loaded up her minivan with as much pet food as we could take, and off we went." She smiled and stroked Jonathan's hair. "I'm blessed with an understanding husband, as well as a mother-in-law who was delighted to have the chance to stay with my children."

Shelby took a breath. "Our church donated gas money, which was a big help, since we drove almost a thousand miles each way."

"And where did you stay?" This was one of Alice's biggest concerns. "If there are no phones, how can I make hotel reservations?"

Shelby's eyebrows rose and she began to laugh. "Oh, Alice, I'm afraid you're going to have to prepare yourself for much more primitive conditions. There are very few hotels open, and those that are not closed are filled with Red Cross workers and medical personnel. Animal rescuers are a bit farther down the totem pole."

"Oh, heavens." Alice felt dismay. "You mean we'll be camping? I haven't camped out in years. I don't even have a sleeping bag, much less a tent or anything to cook on."

"You can borrow my things if you decide to go. I have a six-man tent, a Coleman stove and some cooking gear, a lantern you can hang inside the tent, a two-person air mattress and several sleeping bags. There's a big field behind the kennel area where all the volunteers are pitching their tents."

"But what about bathing?" Alice supposed she had been silly to expect normal accommodations in a disaster zone, but she honestly had not given that aspect of this whole venture much thought.

Shelby shook her head. "Some of the folks rigged up a makeshift shower out of a garden hose surrounded by sheets, but that's it. Oh, and there are two portable potties."

Alice was shocked. "Goodness! I guess I really hadn't thought this through."

"It isn't nearly as bad as it sounds," Shelby hastened to assure her. "It actually was quite a bit of fun. It's not as horribly hot as it could be if it were earlier in the fall, and there aren't many bugs. And honestly, once you get down there and see all those committed people who just showed up because they love animals..." Tears welled in her eyes. "It's truly miraculous, Alice. You can see God's hand at work in a very concrete way. There is a level of selflessness that I have never experienced before in my life."

Alice was moved by Shelby's impassioned words and encouraged by her open expression of faith. A feeling of peace and certainty washed through Alice. The young woman had been placed in her path, via Jane and that news article, for a reason, Alice felt sure. "I'm going to go," she declared. "For days I've been feeling that God has plans for me, that I am supposed to do something to help those animals. So I'm just going to do it."

"That's very much how I felt. And I will be glad I did it for the rest of my life." Shelby wrapped her arm around Jonathan, who had started to fidget.

"You've convinced me. What do I need to take along?"

"I made a list for you on that sheet." Shelby indicated the paper she had handed to Alice earlier. "I also included three Web sites that have bulletin boards where volunteers can share information as well as updates on the animal-rescue efforts. Do you use the Internet?"

"Yes. Well, my sister does. My skills barely cover e-mail." Alice felt compelled to be honest. "Jane is far more able to get around online than I am, so she can help me."

"Is there anyone you've spoken with about going? You shouldn't go alone. It is a disaster area. And you need at least one person to share the driving, especially if you're planning on driving straight through."

Alice immediately thought of Mark Graves. A long-time friend with whom she had been romantically involved during her college days, Mark was the head veterinarian at the Philadelphia Zoo. He might be going down there. Even if he was not, he might know someone who would like to travel with her. "I haven't spoken with anyone yet, but I know someone I can ask. I'm sure I will find someone who'd like to go along." If Mark was not going, Alice thought, she might ask one of the older high school or college students from the Grace Chapel congregation to accompany her.

"Wonderful!" Shelby rose and Jonathan jumped down quickly. "I won't keep you," she looked down at her son, then looked at Alice apologetically. "Please stay in touch and don't hesitate to call if you need more information."

As Alice returned from having seen Shelby and Jonathan out, she heard footsteps in the kitchen. "Hello," she called.

"Hello, Alice. Where are you?" The voice belonged to Jane.

As Alice entered the kitchen, she had to smile. "You match," she told her younger sister.

"Pardon?" Jane looked bewildered. "I match what?"

"The kitchen." Alice gestured around them. She often envied Jane her sense of style and today was no exception. Jane wore a pair of black-and-white houndstooth trousers with a loose and flowing red top decorated with black piping. She looked very much a part of the kitchen, with its colors in a similar theme.

"So I do." Jane laughed. "I swear I didn't do it on purpose."

"Well, regardless, you look very chic. Very put together." Alice shook her head ruefully. "The way I'd love to be if only I had the vision to create a look as easily as you do."

"I think you dress nicely," Jane said loyally. She waved a notebook at Alice. "I accomplished a lot this afternoon."

"Wonderful. You can tell Louise as well as me at dinner. And I have news too. I met with Shelby, the woman who just came back from down South."

"Oh, I bet you have loads to share. But speaking of dinner…" Jane gestured in the direction of the kitchen table. "I need to peel some potatoes and carrots. I'm making a roast tonight."

"I'll set the table and then I'll help." Alice reached for the flatware, then paused. "Would you help me look something up on the Internet tonight, Jane?"

"Sure." Jane already had an apron tied around her trim middle. "We can do it as soon as the dishes are finished."

Chapter Four

*T*he following morning, the three sisters attended church, walking to the picturesque white chapel where their father had been pastor.

As they had the past few Sundays, the members of the congregation said special prayers for the persons harmed and displaced by the recent Florida hurricane. Alice added her own private prayers for the animals that were so much on her mind.

Rev. Kenneth Thompson was normally a riveting speaker; nevertheless, that morning Alice found her concentration lacking. A lamb on one of the beautiful stained-glass window panels caught her attention, and she remembered the sad scene with the little white dog she had seen on the news. Her anticipation rose. She could not wait to get involved in the animal-rescue efforts.

With Jane's help, her Internet foray had borne fruit. Alice found a Web site administered by a large humane organization that provided a great deal of practical information. Volunteers planning a trip or wanting to go south posted their locations and possible dates for travel. Volunteers in many communities posted notes about supplies they had gathered that needed to be taken to the rescue facilities in case anyone driving down had room to spare in a vehicle. Volunteers returning from their animal-rescue experiences posted directions to various rescue areas, information about supplies needed and personal notes that Alice found useful. They included such tips as remembering to bring lots of bug spray, taking sturdy shoes rather than sandals or flip-flops and making sure to bring nonperishable food because there was no refrigeration available. When one woman even suggested that they bring their own toilet tissue, Alice began to wonder if she was rash to be doing this. Then she thought about the animals in such desperate need. Her desire for luxuries and comforts seemed trivial and self-indulgent.

When the congregation rose, Alice started with surprise. Had she completed the service on autopilot? Hastily she rose and flipped through her hymnal to find the selection. As the organ began to play and a familiar tune fell on her ears, Alice could not stop a wide smile from spreading over her face.

The closing hymn was "All Things Bright and Beautiful." Alice felt warm certainty spread through her for a second time as she sang the opening verse: "All things bright and beautiful, / All creatures great and small, / All things wise and wonderful: / The Lord God made them all." God was blessing her endeavor, she felt sure.

As everyone began to file out of the chapel after the service, Alice heard her name called. She looked over to see Jane waving at her.

Jane had begun to chat with June Carter on her way out. "Alice, did you know June is the leader of a feline-rescue group?"

"Good morning, Alice." June was a petite, pleasant, fifty-something woman whose natural blonde hair showed speckles of silver in certain lights. Alice knew June had a college-age daughter and a married son, both of whom lived in the Philadelphia area. A fellow member of the church board, June owned the Coffee Shop on the corner of Chapel Road and Hill Street. She always seemed friendly and warm, although Alice didn't know June well. "Jane tells me you're considering a trip south to work in animal rescue."

Alice nodded. "I'm hoping to leave next week if I can get everything organized." She paused, wondering if June was going to offer to donate some supplies for cats.

"Would you have an extra spot in your car?" June asked.

Alice blinked. "Are you kidding?" Her voice rose in her excitement, a reaction completely at odds with her normal understated demeanor. "I would be thrilled to have company. I've been wondering how I was going to find someone to go with me."

"Wonder no more. I have been thinking I should go down there and help too. When I heard you might be going, I knew God was giving me a kick in the pants."

"I felt the same way. Jane gave me an article she found about a woman from Potterston who has just returned from volunteering. I've spoken with her and I want to do this." She took a deep breath. "It's a little scary, to tell you the truth. I'm nervous about going into a disaster area, nervous about the living conditions, nervous about being away from everyone and everything I've ever known."

"Well, I think it will be a grand adventure. And now you won't be alone."

"How wonderful! We'd better get together so we can make our plans."

"Plans for what?" Louise paused beside them. "Hello, June. How are you?"

"I'm fine." June smiled at Louise. "I'm going to go south with Alice, and I'm so excited already I can barely stand it."

"I'll call you this afternoon," Alice said, smiling at June. "Thank you again so much."

"I'll look forward to it," June said. "Oh, Alice, I just know we're doing the right thing."

Louise moved on ahead, her back straight and her expression rigid. Alice sighed inwardly, realizing that her older sister was not happy with her. She would talk with Louise that afternoon, she vowed. She would try to explain why she felt so compelled to go on this rescue mission.

Other churchgoers hailed Alice as she made her way to the back of the church. She shook Rev. Thompson's hand, relieved when he did not ask her any specific questions about the sermon. As the daughter of a minister, Alice knew how hard he worked to write his homilies. She would hate for him to think that his efforts had not held her interest.

As she started across the sidewalk to where her family was waiting for her, she noticed Ethel had joined Louise and Jane.

"Alice Howard!" Ethel Buckley's stern tone made Alice feel like a grade-schooler about to be called down for misbehavior.

"Hello, Aunt Ethel. Have I done something wrong?"

"Louise tells me you haven't given up this foolish idea to go save animals in Florida. Really, Alice, I'm surprised at you, worrying your family like this. It's a disaster zone. On the news, they say there are people running around at night looting. There are shoot-outs between the National Guard and gangs roaming the area. It wouldn't be safe. Why, I would worry myself sick the whole time you were gone." Ethel took a deep breath, clearly prepared to go on, but Alice leaped into the momentary lull.

"Aunt Ethel. Louise." She held up a hand. "I understand your reservations. I really do. And I appreciate your concern. But my heart is telling me this is the right thing to do. I was thinking of Father yesterday, wondering what he would have said. And do you know what? I believe he would have approved. He always said that each of us has special gifts, that we should use our unique personal skills to help others. Well, I love animals. I may not be a veterinarian, but I do know how to care for creatures in distress, and Father would have encouraged me to use that knowledge. He might have been concerned for my safety, and he might have mentioned his concern, but he wouldn't have continued to try to undermine my decision. Do you know what he would have done?" Alice had tears in her eyes and she swallowed hard before she continued. "He would have prayed for my safety. He would have given my life into Christ's care and trusted that He would be with me throughout the trip. Father would have . . . he would have given me his blessing." Her voice died away to a whisper as Jane put an arm around her shoulders and squeezed gently.

There was a lengthy silence. Alice was aware of a bird in one of the large shade trees that overhung the sidewalk, singing his heart out. She wanted to speak, to apologize for her outburst, but her throat felt constricted.

"Oh, Alice." Ethel sighed. "I'm sorry. I didn't mean to hurt your feelings. And you're exactly right about Daniel. He would have supported your decision."

"And I suppose we should too." Louise's voice was subdued.

Ethel spread her hands and shrugged. "I'll still worry, you know, but I'll try to trust God for your safety."

"I will too," said Louise.

"And I," Jane chimed in, although Alice knew that Jane was simply trying to help smooth over the awkwardness. Her younger sister had been supportive almost from the start, once she'd gotten past her initial reaction.

"Thank you," Alice said, looking at each of them. "Making this trip is very important to me."

❧

The following morning, Alice took the portable telephone from the kitchen and closeted herself in her father's library.

The room was a special refuge for Alice. Her father had used the room as his study during his lifetime, and it still bore signs of his occupancy in items like his books, the framed family photographs on the wall behind his desk and the mahogany box in which he had stored his pen collection. She felt more of her father's presence here than in any other room of the inn, and she often retreated to the study when she was feeling overwhelmed or upset. Today she was not upset and she was not particularly over-whelmed. Nevertheless, she was excited and her fingers trembled as she punched in the telephone number she had looked up in her address book.

"Mark Graves," said a pleasant male voice.

"Hello, Mark. It's Alice."

"Alice! Hello! You must be psychic."

"Why is that?"

"I've been planning to call you, and here you beat me to it. How are you?" When they were in college, Mark's lack of faith had been a major obstacle between them, and ulti-mately their romantic relationship foundered. They remained good friends, although their lives took different directions, and Alice suspected that hearing his voice always would make her heart beat a little faster than usual.

"I'm well," Alice said. "How have you been feeling?"

"Never better."

"I'm glad to hear it." And she was. Mark had suffered a heart attack in recent years, and she worried about how well he was taking care of himself in between their infrequent contacts. "Why were you going to call me?"

"That can wait," Mark said easily. "Why don't you tell me why you called today?"

Alice took a deep breath. "I've been thinking about traveling down to Florida to work with an animal-rescue group. I wanted to get your advice and see if you knew of any places where I might be of help."

There was a momentary silence. Then Mark began to laugh.

"What? What did I say?"

"I should have known." Mark still was chuckling. "We always have been on the same wavelength. Alice, I'm leaving to go to Florida today. I intended to invite you to come down. I know you love animals, and your nurse's training would be invaluable."

"You're leaving today?"

"Yes. The zoo is sending a mobile vet clinic and a team, and I volunteered to go. Don't feel obligated. I almost didn't call because I was afraid to presume on our friendship."

"In what way?"

"You have a good heart. I was afraid you might feel you needed to help even if you couldn't take the time away from work or the inn."

"Time off isn't a problem, but I couldn't possibly leave today." Disappointment shaded her tone.

"I didn't mean that you needed to leave today," he said hastily. "I'm going to be down there for several weeks. I thought perhaps you could round up some volunteers and drive down for a shorter period of time."

"I already have a friend who has agreed to go with me. We were thinking of leaving next Sunday after we have gathered supplies and as many donations as we can carry."

"Excellent!"

"But how will I know where to find you? I understand that cell phone service is all but impossible and land lines aren't going to be restored for some time yet."

"The zoo was contacted by HOUS, the Humane Organization of the United States. Are you familiar with it?"

"Oh yes. I've been donating to them for years. It's a national humane society."

"They have established a rescue site about fifteen miles from the center of the disaster area. It's called Camp Compassion, and they are recruiting as many volunteers as they can find."

"Oh, I've heard about Camp Compassion. A lady from Potterston just came back from there, and I've spoken to her."

"Then you probably know more than I do."

"I doubt that. But I wanted to be well prepared. I've never gone into a disaster area before, and the prospect makes me slightly nervous."

"Tell you what. I'll e-mail you everything I know before I leave today. Directions, lists of things you'll need, that kind of thing."

"That would be wonderful. I got some information from the Internet, too, but one never knows how accurate that is. Could you also send me a list of veterinary and pet supplies that would be useful? My friend June and I are planning to solicit donations this week."

"I'll be happy to e-mail you a list. Would you be willing to bring some things down from the zoo if I have them sent to you?"

"Of course." Then she thought she had better qualify that. "Exactly how much are we talking about here?"

"Could you handle two large boxes?"

"Oh. Of course." She had feared he meant significantly more than that.

"You're amazing," Mark said, and the note in his voice brought warmth to Alice's cheeks. She was thankful he could not see her.

"All right, then," she said briskly. "I'll see you next week. We're planning to leave right after church on Sunday and drive straight through so we expect to arrive sometime mid to late Monday."

"Terrific. I'll see you then. Have a safe trip."

"You, too, Mark. I'll be praying for you."

"And I you. Good-bye, Alice. God bless you."

As she hung up the telephone, Alice could not help thinking of Mark's final words. Since his heart attack, Mark's spirit had been opened. He was striving to learn all he could about walking a Christian path.

"Thank You, Lord," she whispered.

Tuesday morning, Louise helped Jane and Alice fix breakfast for their four guests. Afterward, she was preparing for the three piano students she would be teaching that afternoon when the telephone rang. Jane just had returned from soliciting items for the upcoming crafts fair, and Alice had run to the store to purchase a few odds and ends they needed, so Louise reached for the telephone on the reception desk.

"Grace Chapel Inn, Louise speaking. May I help you?"

"Louise, this is Kenneth Thompson. Do you have a few moments to brainstorm with me?"

"Of course."

"Have you met Kettil and Karin Lindars?"

"The new people who just joined the church? They came from Minneapolis, didn't they?"

"Yes. They have five children, although the two elder daughters are in college now, I believe." Kenneth cleared his throat. "Karin approached me last week with an idea I thought sounded quite interesting. Have you ever heard of a Santa Lucia festival?"

"Oh yes." Louise chuckled. "Well, in a very superficial manner. One of my students has a doll that she takes everywhere with her. One of its outfits is a dress—a nightgown, really—for a Santa Lucia festival. It even has a wreath of greens with candles sticking up from it and a tray of some kind of goodies that apparently are part of the celebration."

"That's right!" Kenneth sounded as if Louise were a student who'd just won the spelling bee. "It's a Swedish tradition. Apparently, in the Lindars' old community in Minnesota, there was a large population of Swedish ancestry, and they held a Santa Lucia festival every year."

"Oh no, you don't," said Louise as the light dawned. "I'm already helping Aunt Ethel with the crafts fair."

"No, you're not, you fibber." He laughed. "Jane is. I heard all about how Alice and you wriggled out of it."

"Well, I *am* helping on the day of the fair."

"This is a musical endeavor. You are such a valuable resource that you're the first person I thought of. Really,

Louise, this wouldn't take much of your time. Please consider it."

"What, exactly, are you asking me to do?"

"Plan a Santa Lucia celebration with Karin Lindars. Guide her. Lead rehearsals. Her children have done it every year, so she can tell you what should be included. Her two oldest daughters have each represented Lucia, and her youngest daughter has been very upset since they moved that she would not get to play the role. I thought it might help her daughter to feel happier about the move if she had something familiar to bridge the chasm between her life in Minnesota and her life here. If it goes well this year, we might consider making it a Grace Chapel tradition."

"And when would it be held?"

"It normally occurs on the Sunday closest to December 13, which would be Sunday the fifteenth, but the craft show is Saturday the fourteenth, so I thought we could have it during the Sunday school hour on Sunday the eighth."

Louise took a moment to process all those "Sundays" in one sentence. "And you're asking me to plan it?"

"And conduct rehearsals. Karin said she would be happy to help. She has suggestions for music and additional activities, but she's a quiet person and isn't comfortable doing this all on her own."

It sounded interesting. And working with Karin would be a nice opportunity to get to know a new church member. "All right. Do you have the Lindars' phone number?"

Rev. Thompson gave her the telephone number and they said their farewells. Then Louise walked briskly to the kitchen, where she knew she probably could find Jane. Just as she had thought, Jane sat at the table surrounded by a sea of notes scribbled on all sizes and shapes of paper.

"Jane, what on earth are you doing?"

Jane looked up. "Organizing my notes for the crafts fair." She grimaced. "Each time I spoke to someone, I scribbled down the information and stuck it in a folder. Now I have to put it all into some kind of order." She sat up straighter. "You're a wonderful organizer, Louise. Could you help me?"

"I'd be glad to, in exchange for a favor from you. Could you help me look up something on the computer?"

"Of course. What are you trying to find?" Jane rose from the table and headed for the reception desk in the front hall.

"I need information on the Santa Lucia festival."

"The what?"

"Santa Lucia festival," Louise repeated as her sister began to type. "Kenneth has asked me to help put together a little program to honor Santa Lucia, also known as St. Lucy, who was a Christian martyr of the fifth century. A celebration is held in Scandinavian countries every year."

"I'm going to start charging research fees," Jane said jokingly. "First Alice and now you. The next thing I know, it'll be Aunt Ethel in here asking me to look up something for her. There." She pointed at the screen. "On the left is a list of Web sites that have information about the Santa Lucia thingy. You click on one and the Web site will open in the window on the right. If you see useful information, just click on the little printer up at the top and print out the pages."

"Sounds simple enough. But don't go far, just in case."

Twenty minutes later, Louise had a small stack of paper and more information on St. Lucy and the celebration than she would ever need to know.

"*Lucia* means 'light,'" she announced as she entered the kitchen, where Jane had put away her notes and was expertly rolling out piecrusts. Louise's attention was diverted. "What kind of pie are you making?"

"Cherry. Remember those sour cherries I canned? When I went into the pantry to get some of the tomatoes we put up last summer, I saw them and immediately had a hankering for cherry pie."

"I adore cherry pie, especially yours. I volunteer to be your taste-tester again."

Jane chuckled. "And here I thought I'd have to do it myself. How generous of you, Louie! So tell me how you made out on your quest for information."

"Wonderfully, thanks to you." Louise waved the sheaf of papers. "Santa Lucia's Day is celebrated across Scandinavia on December 13, marking the beginning of the holiday season. In one version, Lucia is said to have been a Christian virgin martyred for her beliefs. According to the story, she angered the man to whom she was betrothed when she gave away most of her wealth to the poor. In another, she is said to have carried food to Christians hiding in dark underground catacombs in the days of early Christian persecution in Rome. To light the way as she carried the food, she wore a wreath of candles on her head. Without doing a lot more research, I don't know exactly what the truth may be, but I do know the Santa Lucia festival is a recent celebration."

"How recent?"

"Early twentieth century."

"Wow! Even more recent than Thanksgiving or the Fourth of July."

"Much more so." Louise read from one of the papers she held. "There are many legends about her, and in each one Lucia stands as a symbol of light and hope to all humankind. Santa Lucia's Day begins the feasting, merriment, singing and the spirit of friendliness and goodwill that lasts all through the holidays.'"

"I guess the 'feasting, merriment and singing' is where you come in. Did Kenneth give you any specific details?"

"No, but I found a number of things in the research. And don't forget I'll have Mrs. Lindars' suggestions as well."

Alice came into the kitchen midway through Louise's explanation and so Louise repeated the request from Rev. Thompson.

"That's wonderful. I'll be back in plenty of time. I'd hate to miss our first Santa Lucia celebration."

Jane's hands paused for a moment and she looked up. "So you've definitely decided to go?"

"Yes. I spoke to Mark Graves, and he's also going down to Florida. We'll be there at the same time." Alice went on, telling her sisters the details of her plans.

"Well, I'm relieved that Mark will be there too," Louise said. "And Alice, I feel I owe you another apology. I never should have said anything to Aunt Ethel yesterday."

"Thank you. But it's all right, Louise. My trip isn't a secret. Aunt Ethel had to know sometime."

"So you're leaving on Sunday and returning the following weekend?"

Alice confirmed her plans with a nod.

"Well, don't worry about anything here. I'll help Jane with the inn as much as possible."

"Fortunately, we aren't terribly busy," Jane said. "You will be back for Thanksgiving, Alice, won't you?"

"Of course. Can you imagine me willingly missing out on your pumpkin pie?"

Jane laughed. "I'll be sure to make plenty."

Chapter Five

W ednesday, Alice awoke with butterfly wings
beating madly inside her. Time was flying by as
she made preparations for her trip to Camp Compassion.

Late Monday afternoon, she had called Carlene Moss,
owner of the local newspaper, the *Acorn Nutshell*, and
Carlene interviewed June and Alice at the newspaper office
Tuesday. Carlene intended to run an article in the paper,
which came out once a week on Wednesday, and Alice
hoped it might generate a few donations to add to the small
store of items and financing she and June had received so
far.

As she was making up the bed in the Sunrise Room for
a Michigan couple scheduled to arrive that afternoon, she
heard the telephone ring.

"Grace Chapel Inn, Alice speaking. May I help you?"
She enjoyed taking telephone calls from people making
reservations. She always experienced a sense of anticipation
about what the new guests might be like. She enjoyed asking where they had heard about the inn and if there were

any special dietary requests or anything else necessary to make their stay comfortable. It felt so…so professional.

Alice recognized that she had a valuable and satisfying career in nursing. And she once had a valuable and satisfying life with her father, to which her fond memories and the ache that still haunted her heart occasionally could testify. But this was different. She really could not explain it.

"Is this Alice Howard from the newspaper?" The voice was older, female and haughty.

"I—I suppose it is." She had not seen the weekly paper yet, but she was looking forward to learning what the reporter said about the trip she and June were planning. Apparently, this lady already had read it.

"Miss Howard, my name is Emmaline Daughtry. I would like a little more information about exactly what you intend to do if you travel down to this Camp Compassion place."

Alice's eyebrows rose. "Ms. Daughtry—"

"Mrs." She said it as if she were royalty, and Alice had to smile.

"I beg your pardon. Mrs. Daughtry, my friend June and I have spoken with a woman who recently returned, as well as with a veterinarian who is traveling down to work there now. Both of them assure us that there is ample work to be done. I cannot speak to the exact type of work, although I assume most of it will be unskilled labor. I love animals, but I am not trained to work with them. If you have seen the same things on the news programs that I have, you have seen how desperate the need is. I'll do whatever they need me to do. Feed, walk, rescue. Whatever they need."

"I wish to make a donation, Miss Howard. How do you intend to get to this place?"

"We'll be driving, ma'am."

"Well then, you're going to need gas. If you're prepared to offer your hard work, the least those of us at home can do is help you financially." Mrs. Daughtry then named a sum that caused Alice's mouth to open in utter disbelief. "Use what you need for transportation, and if there's any left over, I would like you to donate it to the camp to use for food and shelter."

"Mrs. Daughtry, I don't know what to say. I can assure you there will be plenty left over—"

"Good. Now, I'm concerned that if I put this in the mail it may not arrive before you leave. Is there any way that someone could pick it up in the next few days? I live in Potterston, which I realize is out of your way."

"Oh no, ma'am, that's not a problem. I'll be happy to stop by this week on my way to work. I'll call first." Alice hardly could believe her ears. Even if the article in the paper yielded no other results, this one donation would be a wonderful gift to offer the camp.

♀

Jane again had her notes for the crafts fair spread out on the kitchen table when Alice came through the door after work. She immediately jumped up and grabbed the newspaper from the counter. "Your article is in the paper!"

"Yes, I heard. I already received one call about a donation." Alice pressed a hand to her heart. "The paper wasn't delivered by the time I left for work. I'm afraid to look. Do June and I sound rash for rushing off on an ill-advised journey?"

Jane had to laugh. "Not at all," she assured Alice. "It's a lovely article. I predict lots of donations," she said as she passed the newspaper to her sister.

"We've already had an amazing start." Alice explained Mrs. Daughtry's telephone call to Jane.

Jane whistled, impressed. "That's awesome. You just never know what the good Lord is going to provide, do you? You look tired. How was your shift?"

Alice shook her head with a wry smile. "Interesting. One of my dementia patients got out of her gown and went wandering down to the first floor before anyone realized she was gone."

"Oh my! I bet that startled more than a few people. The poor woman. She would be mortified if she knew. Will she remember it?"

Alice shook her head. "Thankfully, no."

"I thought people with dementia usually go to nursing homes."

"Yes, but they get ill like anyone else. Actually, probably more often. Flu and pneumonia can tear through a nursing home like that hurricane ripped through Florida."

Jane shivered. "That's awful. Is it wrong of me to pray that I never get to the point that I have to go to a home?"

"I believe God understands. We all have a fear of that." Alice indicated the papers on which Jane was working. "New recipes?"

"Crafts fair. I have a nice assortment of things lined up for the church to sell. And you won't believe it, but Florence is organizing about half of it."

"How did you manage that? At the board meeting, she was positive it could never succeed."

Jane shrugged. "Honestly, I think she was simply suffering from hurt feelings. I tried to make her feel as if I valued her opinion—which I do—and she became very helpful. In fact, there are only two more things yet to confirm."

"What are those?"

"I need to ask the Sunday school teachers if their classes would be willing to make up packages of 'Christmas Cocoa.' I found a really cute idea in a magazine. You make a blend of powdered cocoa, cinnamon and a few other spices and place enough for a one-serving drink in a sandwich bag. You add a little cellophane twist of marshmallows and a candy cane and then punch a hole at the top of the bag for ribbon. Before tying the ribbon, you attach a holly leaf tag with instructions on it."

"Very cute and very inexpensive," Alice murmured. "Especially if a group volunteers to work on it. It's a perfect project for the children."

"Speaking of perfect projects for children—" Jane began.

"I know, I know. You want the ANGELs to make macramé bracelets."

"How did you know that?" Jane was surprised.

"News travels fast in this town. I'll be happy to organize it, Jane, but I will have to get someone else to actually oversee the project, since I'll be away."

"Maybe one of the mothers would help."

"I'll check and let you know." Alice paused before heading upstairs to change out of her work clothes. "Were there any packages for me today?"

"Oh!" Jane sprang out of her chair. "Thank you for reminding me. The UPS man brought two boxes. I put them in the front hall because I didn't know what else to do with them." She led the way to the front of the house. "I think they're from Mark. What on earth do you think he sent you?"

"Relax, matchmaker." Alice laughed. "It's only supplies for me to take to him in Florida." Then she caught sight of the boxes. "Good heavenly days! Mark must think we have a U-Haul trailer." The boxes were at least three feet square, wrapped in brown paper and heavily taped.

"I feel so much better knowing that Mark is going to be in Florida." Jane waggled her eyebrows knowingly at her older sister. "And you're going to meet him there."

"Oh, Jane, it's not like that and you know it!" Alice was exasperated but she had to laugh. "True, I do still find Mark attractive, but it's not as if we're planning to elope. We're going south to make a difference in the suffering of so many poor animals. I doubt there will be a lot of time for socializing, and I can't imagine the atmosphere will be remotely romantic."

"One can always hope," Jane retorted, turning to go back to the kitchen.

⌒

Louise did not sleep well. Thoughts of the Christmas crafts fair had marched incessantly through her head. She tossed and turned.

She awoke late on Thursday, feeling as tired as if she had just completed an exhausting piano concert on which she'd worked for months.

What if the fair was a disaster? How could Ethel possibly plan a successful event in little more than a month? Why had she ever opened her mouth to suggest that it be a Christmas event?

Louise made her bed, showered, then dressed in a classic navy skirt with a white sweater set. As she fastened her pearls around her neck, she reminded herself that her intentions had been good. She had been thinking long-term. How in the world could she have known that Ethel would consider attempting it this year?

When she went down into the kitchen, Alice and Jane had already finished with breakfast. Jane was tracing a holly leaf pattern onto dark green construction paper, and Alice was carefully cutting out the leaf outlines.

"I can't believe she's seriously trying to pull this off," Louise announced to her sisters.

Jane's hands stilled halfway around the leaf. Today she wore a hunter-green tunic over ivory wool slacks. The silhouette of an old woodstove was appliquéd to the tunic.

Alice, more casually dressed in jeans and a tan sweater, stopped just as she was about to begin cutting another leaf.

Carefully, she set down her scissors. "Who might 'she' be, and what might we be discussing?"

"Oh, sorry." Louise served herself some of the cream-cheese coffee cake Jane had made yesterday and pulled out a chair at the table. Jane had placed a cheery arrangement of yellow and white mums in a cut-glass container on the table, but its beauty was lost on Louise. "I didn't sleep well. How could Aunt Ethel think that trying to pull together a crafts fair in a few short weeks is a good idea? She clearly doesn't have any idea—"

"This is Aunt Ethel you're talking about," Jane reminded her, going back to her tracing. "The woman has more energy than the three of us put together."

"And," said Alice, "she has a certain way of making things happen."

"Yes, but—"

"Why don't you give her a call after you have some breakfast?" Jane suggested. "Share your worries with her. Maybe she's having second thoughts about attempting it, and she just needs to hear someone else voice concern."

"You're just hoping you don't have to gather a whole lot of crafts."

"I'll have you know I already did gather quite a selection." Jane gestured to the holly leaves. "Alice and I are getting some things done for a project the Sunday school classes have agreed to take on."

Ordinarily, Louise believed in eating slowly. She believed it to be better for the digestion. But today she raced through her breakfast, then called Ethel. Luckily, her aunt was home and was more than happy to talk about the crafts fair with Louise.

Shortly before nine, Louise left the inn and walked briskly along the flagstone path to the carriage house, where her aunt had lived for the past decade.

Ethel opened the door the moment Louise stepped onto the small front porch. "Good morning, Louise. Please come in. I'm happy to entertain any ideas for the crafts fair."

"I don't really have ideas," Louise hastened to explain. "I've been thinking more along the lines of all the logistical things that have to happen in order for this to succeed. Aunt Ethel, are you still sure you want to tackle this in such a short span of time?"

"Of course I'm sure. Sit down, dear, and tell me what you're concerned about. What can I get you to drink? Would you like a little snack?"

"Oh, I'm fine. I just finished breakfast. But thank you for the offer." Louise took a seat on the couch, laying her jacket over the back of the nearby rocking chair. So much for trying to talk her aunt into waiting until next year. Louise had heard that tone of voice before, the one that meant Ethel had no intention of backing down. She took a deep breath. "Well. Let's talk money first. What is your budget for food and planning?"

"But I'm on the board," Ethel said blithely. "I know what the church's budget can handle."

"All right." Louise could see that she was getting nowhere fast. "What do you plan to do about advertising?"

"Advertising?" Ethel made it sound like a word from a foreign tongue.

"You might try to get the newspapers to do an article for you since it's the first time you're trying it and it's a charitable event. That would save actually placing an ad, which would add to your expenses."

"A newspaper article." Ethel nodded. "That's a very good idea, Louise. Is there anything else you can think of?"

Louise was just scratching the surface. "You'll need boxes to be decorated and set in front of each raffle item, and you'll have to make a sign advertising the raffle. You'll also have to make a sign for the baked-goods table, so people understand all the proceeds from that will go to Helping Hands and not into some stranger's pocket. And you'll need a price list for the baked goods."

"I can have someone make one."

Louise nodded her head slowly, telling herself all she had to do was plant the seed. "All right. How about change?"

"Change? What would we want to change at this point?"

"No, Aunt Ethel, not *changing things*. I mean money. You need change in case your customers hand you large bills."

"All right, Louise. You've made your point." Ethel rose and walked into her small kitchen, returning a moment later with a folder and a pen. She made a production out of opening the folder and extracting a notepad, then crossed one leg over the other and said, "I'm taking notes, so I can write down anything I haven't already considered."

"Well, if you plan to sell drinks and sandwiches, you'll want to ask around to see who can give you the best prices. Some of the ladies from the social circle might make soup if you asked them to, but you need some kind of sandwiches."

Ethel made a dismissive motion. "I'll get a tray of turkey and ham."

Oh dear. Louise's anxiety level reached a new high. "I don't think you want to purchase an arranged tray, Aunt Ethel. That's costly. See if you can get a bargain from a butcher or deli. You might even get a better price on the meat over in Potterston," she mused.

Ethel was scribbling madly, but she paused at that suggestion and looked up. "I couldn't do that to the Acorn Hill merchants," she said in a shocked tone. "I like to keep my shopping in the community. If everyone goes somewhere else to shop, small businesses like those in our little town won't be able to stay open."

"I agree, but this isn't your personal shopping you're talking about. You want to spend as little as possible so that when all the proceeds are matched against the initial outlay, you will make a nice profit to donate to Helping Hands."

"Louise, I am not willing to ignore our local shops just for the sake of a few dollars." Ethel's tone was quite definite.

Louise took a deep breath. "Perhaps you are right. Let's move on. We need to figure out how many volunteers will be needed in each area and how long their shifts should be."

"Oh, I thought I'd have sign-up sheets at our next Seniors Social Circle meeting."

Louise sighed. She so wanted the seniors' group to make a success of this. If it didn't go well, Ethel might never get a second chance. Louise took another deep, fortifying breath and a long moment to compose herself. *Lord*, she thought, *give me patience. Aunt Ethel's heart is in the right place.* "I think you'd do better with more structure," she said.

"Oh, I'm sure the ladies in the Seniors Social Circle will be willing to work the whole day, just like I am. After all, this is for a good cause."

Momentarily speechless, Louise gazed at her aunt. Searching for tact, she said, "That might be expecting a bit much. After all, you are in far better health than many of your friends."

"Yes, I suppose I am." Ethel preened, pleased by Louise's statement. Then she frowned. "But we'll have to work to find enough people to fill all those hours. I wonder if Alice's ANGELs are old enough to be reliable assistants."

"Perhaps with the food and the raffle, but we hardly could ask them to oversee the vendors."

"Oh well." Ethel shrugged. "The good Lord will help us make this happen."

It sounded very much like what Alice had described her aunt saying at the board meeting. "I hope so." Louise's comment was heartfelt.

"Thank you for your suggestions, Louise." Ethel set down her pencil. "I'll add them to my list of ideas to consider."

Louise raised one eyebrow. Ideas? As far as she was concerned, the things she had said were imperatives.

"There's more," she said grimly, determined to give her aunt all the information she could. "Have you thought about how to measure and lay out the space for the booths? You really should measure the Assembly Room."

"Oh, I've decided not to use the Assembly Room," Ethel said breezily. "I think that we'll set up several large tents outside. We can make it a real community event, with face painting and party hats for the children, and hot apple cider—"

"Outside? It is going to be *cold* in December!"

"I beg your pardon?" Ethel said, raising her eyebrows.

"I'm sorry," Louise began. "I don't mean to be rude. But I do not think you realize the scope—"

"You can't stand not to be in charge, Louise," Ethel said. "I know you'd love to take over this crafts fair and show everyone how much better you could organize it."

The attack was so unfair that Louise did not even know how to respond. She opened her mouth, then closed it again. For the first time in quite a while, she felt the sting of tears behind her eyelids.

"I want you to succeed and I've been worrying myself sleepless," she said calmly. She said another prayer for patience before continuing. "I thought that I could give you some guidance since I have experience with this kind of endeavor. I was wrong. I apologize." She turned and began striding for the door, grabbing her coat without a pause and sailing out onto the porch.

"Louise?" She heard a tremble in her elderly aunt's voice, but Louise didn't trust herself to speak kindly, so she kept going down the steps and across the flagstones.

Chapter Six

*T*he walk back to the inn from the carriage house took less than a minute, not nearly long enough to calm down. Louise was still seething when she stepped through the kitchen door.

Jane, at the sink, took one look at her face and picked up a platter full of brownies. She held them out to Louise. "Oh dear. It didn't go well?"

Louise did not respond. It was an indication to Jane of just how upset her eldest sister was. Louise took a brownie, then sank down into a chair at the table, miming banging her head against the wood.

Alice was still at the table, gluing instructions for the Christmas Cocoa mix onto the holly leaves she had cut out. She rose and stood behind Louise. "Take a deep breath." She placed a hand on her sister's back and rubbed small circles. "Try to relax a bit. Then you can tell us all about it. Sharing a burden can lighten your load."

In this case, Louise wasn't so sure about that. But she drew a napkin out of the holder near the center of the table and laid down her brownie. "Thank you," she said, looking up as Jane set a glass of cold cider in front of her.

"I would have made tea, but you already have steam coming out of your ears."

"Very funny." But Louise was beginning to feel a little calmer.

Alice pulled out a chair at the end of the table and sat, picking up the cider Jane also had poured for her. "So how bad was it?"

Louise just shook her head. "I feel as if I've just returned from talking to a wall. Aunt Ethel seemed determined to ignore every sensible suggestion I made."

"Did she say she didn't like your ideas?"

"She never said that." In all fairness, Louise could not say that Ethel had disliked the things she'd said. "But she resisted me every step of the way. And just as I finished, she got angry and accused me of wanting to take over her position as chairman." She huffed. "As if."

Jane was agog. "Are you kidding? She didn't."

"She most certainly did." Louise was getting revved up just thinking about it again.

Alice reached over and patted Louise's arm. "Oh, Louise, I'm so sorry. But you know how she is. It's very important to her to feel needed and necessary. Her feelings get hurt over the tiniest imagined slight, and she can make a mountain *range* out of a little *ant* hill."

Louise had to laugh at Alice's twist on the cliché.

"No wonder she and Florence are such a volatile mix," Jane commented. "They both need to be handled with kid gloves."

"What, exactly, did she say?" Alice asked.

Louise told them. "I felt as if I was about five years old again, being fussed at. I was intimidated by Aunt Ethel when I was little. She seemed so stern."

"Louise, I'm sorry," Jane said, dropping a dishtowel on the table as she flopped into a seat. "This is my fault."

"Your fault? What do you mean?"

"I'm the one who suggested you offer your pearls of wisdom to Aunt Ethel. I know how she is. I should have thought about how she would react."

"It's nobody's fault," Alice said firmly. "Families have misunderstandings and disagreements. It's part of the package. This, too, shall pass."

Louise knew her sister was right. But Ethel's accusations still stung. She knew she would have to talk with her aunt again. But it would be a few days before she could imagine initiating another conversation.

"Grace Chapel Inn, Alice speaking. May I help you?"

"Hello, Alice, it's June. Again." It was Friday afternoon, and the two women had talked at least a dozen times over the past two days as donations had begun to roll in at a surprising rate.

Alice laughed. "It's a good thing the phone company doesn't charge us by the call, or you and I would be in the poorhouse."

"I know," agreed June. "But I forgot to ask you if you have a large cooler we could take."

"June," said Alice patiently, "I live with a chef. Of course I have a cooler. If you'd like to come over, you can choose the size you want."

"I can't come over right now. A neighbor called. She has six cases of canned dog food she wants to donate."

"Six *cases*?"

"That's what I said. Apparently she bought in bulk because it was cheaper, but her dog is allergic to beef and can't eat it."

"How on earth are we going to fit all these donations into that SUV you borrowed? I know it's big, but still . . ." June had finagled the loan of an enormous used Chevrolet SUV from Moe Burdock, a dealer in Potterston from whom she had bought a number of previous vehicles. She had driven trucks with horse trailers before, so the prospect of driving the SUV didn't bother her. The auto's size made Alice considerably more nervous, but she figured she could handle it on the highway as long as she didn't have to try to parallel park.

"I borrowed a turtle from my son. That should help."

"A turtle? Do you mean one of those luggage carriers that fit on the top of a vehicle?"

"Right. It's the largest size they make, and it will hold a lot."

"Whew! For a moment there I took you literally."

June laughed. "We'd be taking animals in the wrong direction, then, wouldn't we? Also, Moe gave me a flatbed that fits into the trailer hitch on the truck. It's like a big tray, and anything we stow there would have to be boxed and waterproof because it wouldn't be protected from the elements, but it would provide some more space."

"By the time we're done loading, we're going to be getting five miles to the gallon." Consumption of natural resources was something Alice tried hard to be conscious of. Her blue Toyota got more than twenty miles to the gallon around town.

"Not quite that bad, but close."

"I'm glad you called," Alice told her traveling companion. "I was about to call you. The mail was delivered a few minutes ago, and you will never believe what arrived."

"More money?"

"Yes. Checks and cash totaling four hundred dollars."

"Gracious. People certainly have been generous. I admit that when we did the article, I wasn't expecting these kinds of results."

"Add that to what we've already received, and we have more than a thousand dollars. It makes me feel very humble that people trust us to use their money well."

"I'll have to write you a check for the money that I've been given. I deposited it into my checking account because all the checks were made out to me and it made me nervous having them in the house."

"I'll deposit this too," Alice said. "Then I can set aside some money for our expenses and write the director of the camp one large check when we arrive. I don't even know who to make it out to yet."

"Moe's sales manager gave me a donation to be used for gas for our trip," June told her. "It's an Exxon card good for one hundred dollars. That means more of Mrs. Daughtry's donation can go straight to Camp Compassion."

"God certainly has moved people's hearts to respond to this."

"I know. Now why don't we go over what we need to take one more time?"

June was the most organized trip planner Alice ever had met. The two women glanced over their notes yet another time. Alice pulled out a sheet of paper. "I also have a list of all the veterinary supplies that have been donated. They're going to fill at least five boxes, I believe."

"This sounds impressive," June said as Alice proceeded to read down the column.

"I know. But I'm afraid it's going to be a drop in the bucket compared to the needs that exist. I have been reading the daily Internet postings from some of the rescue groups that are getting reports out. There must be thousands of animals down there."

"I know." June's voice was gentle. "But we will have to focus on helping as many as we can."

Alice felt a renewed sense of purpose. "We leave in only two days. Oh, I can't wait!"

"I can't either." June's voice was filled with the same excitement Alice felt. "This is going to be such an adventure!"

After she and June said good-bye, Alice had one more telephone call to make. Britt Nilsen was the mother of one of Alice's former ANGELs. She had helped with the girls' projects in the past, and Alice was hoping she would agree to oversee the bracelet-making in Alice's absence.

Britt and her daughter Ingrid both were at home, and Britt said she would be happy to help with the bracelets. Ingrid overheard the conversation and Alice could hear her high voice chattering away in the background.

"Ingrid wants me to tell you that she has a book with a number of different designs in it. She and her friends do this all the time, you know."

Alice smiled. "I know." She had seen Ingrid wearing rope bracelets many times. It was one of the reasons she had volunteered to have her ANGELs help make the crafts.

"I have a huge bag of embroidery floss that I picked up at a yard sale in September," Britt said. "How about if I donate that to the crafts fair, and we'll use it to make the bracelets?"

Alice was touched by yet another example of generosity. She had a strong feeling that the Lord was moving people to support both her trip and Ethel's crafts fair. "Thank you, Britt. That's a wonderful idea." *And thank You, God, for helping us to make these ministries happen.*

Louise had invited Karin Lindars to come to the inn for their first Santa Lucia planning session on Saturday. The doorbell rang precisely at two. Louise took a moment to turn her pearls so that the clasp was behind her neck where it belonged. Then she walked to the front door and pulled it open.

"Hello." She smiled warmly at the willowy woman who stood on the welcome mat. She offered her hand. "I'm Louise Smith. Please come in."

"I'm Karin Lindars." Tentatively, Karin shook Louise's hand. She was a tall, blue-eyed blonde with porcelain skin. "I've seen you at church with your sisters. And I want to thank you so much for volunteering to plan this celebration."

Although she hadn't exactly volunteered, Louise graciously said, "You're welcome. It sounds quite interesting."

She took the younger woman's coat and hung it on the antique beech coat tree that her father had purchased many years before. Then she led her guest into the dining room. "This is a bit informal, but I thought we might like to sit at the table to take notes. Please have a seat."

Karin pulled out a chair as she looked around at the lovely ivory-and-green room, moving a gentle hand over the gleaming mahogany table. "This is a lovely room. And oh, Swedish mints!" She pointed at the dish of white, pink and green mints that Jane always kept on the dining table.

Louise chuckled. "Believe it or not, I didn't plan that. The care and feeding of our guests is my sister Jane's bailiwick. She keeps those dishes filled on a regular basis." She pulled out a chair and sat at the end of the table at a right angle to Karin, pulling toward her the notepad that she had laid out earlier. "So. Where shall we begin?"

"I'm not really sure." Karin looked distressed, and her pretty blue eyes showed concern. "Food? Music? Oh, it just overwhelms me."

"Now, now," said Louise in a parody of her own no-nonsense teacher voice. "There will be no overwhelming here today. It simply isn't allowed."

Karin smiled, as Louise had intended. "Do you have an idea where to start?" she asked hopefully.

Louise hitched her chair forward. "First, why don't we list the major elements of the event?" She wrote a Roman numeral one on her notepad. "Music. I always think of that first since I am a music teacher by profession. And food. We'll have some kind of light refreshments after the service, I imagine. What else?"

"The service itself?"

Louise wrote it down. "And the children will need costumes, I presume."

"Yes. How many rehearsals shall we have?"

Louise consulted a calendar lying nearby. "I thought three and a dress rehearsal the day before. Will that be enough? All we really need to do is teach the music and select children for any readings."

"That's exactly how we did it in Minnesota." Karin pronounced the name of the state like a true native:

Min-ne-SO-da, although it was lightly overlaid with the Swedish accent that flavored her speech. Louise thought it was charming.

"Did your parents emigrate from Sweden?" she asked.

"No," said Karin, surprising her. "My husband and I did. We grew up in Sweden in the same little town. But after he went to university, he was offered a job overseas... so here we are."

"You speak English so well," Louise said. "Did you take lessons when you were growing up?"

"My mother is American. She went to Sweden with a friend on a summer visit and met my father. They traveled back and forth a few times to meet each other's families and were married the following spring."

"What a wonderful story!"

Karin laughed. "I always thought it was terribly romantic when I was growing up. My daughters, who have lived here all their lives, think she was crazy to give up her whole life to be with him."

"Just wait until they fall in love. Someday they'll meet a man for whom they would leave their families and travel far away."

"So I keep telling them. But I hope they won't find love too soon. Annika, our eldest daughter, has just begun her junior year of college and Kerstin, the second eldest, is a freshman this year."

"How old are your other three? I've seen your youngest daughter and two boys with you at church."

"Marit is fourteen. Our first son, Niklas, is eleven and our youngest, Mattias, is nine."

"That must be a quiet house you have."

Both women laughed.

"I suppose we better get back to business," Louise said. "Now that we know the elements we need to plan, we can get more specific."

"Let's do food first. That one, I know something about."

Louise turned a page and began a list as Karin continued. "Most important are the *Lussekatter*, or Lucia buns. Translated literally, it means, 'Lucia cats,' because they can be shaped like curled-up cats with raisins for eyes. They're glazed saffron buns with raisins, baked in any of several traditional shapes."

"Sounds delicious. I wonder if my sister Jane can come up with a recipe."

"Oh, I have one I'm happy to share. Will she be helping with baking?"

Louise grinned. "Yes, although she doesn't know it yet."

"We might also want to serve ginger cookies or gingerbread, apples or some type of apple food, and coffee. We could add hot chocolate for the children since American children usually are not fond of coffee."

Louise was scribbling quickly. "Excellent. How about costumes? And what, exactly, does St. Lucia do?"

"She will accompany the children to the front of the church and lead them in singing. In our old church, she also carried a candle and a lit candelabra when she got to the front."

"Real fire?" That notion worried Louise.

"Only the one candle carried by the *Lussibrud*—Lucy bride," Karin explained as she saw Louise's eyebrows rise in question. "The five lights in her crown and all the lights carried by the handmaidens can be electric candles.

That relieved Louise significantly. She made more notes. "And you said something about white gowns?"

"Yes. All the girls wear simple white gowns, and the boys can wear either white gowns or long white shirts. The Lucia wears the crown of greens and lights and a red sash. The other girls become the handmaidens and can have belts and crowns of tinsel. The boys are "star boys." They carry wands with stars on the ends."

"Okay. That sounds manageable. We have a few mothers in the congregation who might be willing to help with costuming if their own children are involved. Let's move on to the service. Is there anything in particular you can think of that is done?"

"Gospel readings about the Light of the World. Shall I e-mail my former pastor and ask him for a list?"

"That would be very helpful."

"I'll also ask about the traditional songs and any other special readings he might recommend. We might also want to add some Christmas carols."

"How long do you envision this service will be?"

Karin looked uncertain. "I'm not sure. It seems as if it was fairly short. Perhaps forty minutes?"

"That sounds workable." Louise consulted her list. "I'll wait to select music until you hear from your pastor. We certainly have enough to get started with."

"How should we inform the congregation? We need children to participate," Karin pointed out.

"I'll ask Rev. Thompson to make an announcement at church tomorrow, and I'll write a short note to go in next week's bulletin. If we have a poor turnout at the first rehearsal, then we'll start beating the bushes."

Alice had thought Sunday would never arrive, but finally it did. She and June sat together during the service, and Rev. Thompson gave them an opportunity to address the congregation in order to share details of their upcoming mission and to ask for prayer.

After the service, Alice was approached by many of her fellow parishioners, who promised to support her with daily prayer. She knew how vital that underpinning was, and she profusely thanked them all.

Out of the corner of her eye, Alice noticed Louise standing with one of her piano students' mothers, making small talk. Her back was to the sanctuary, but she was angled just enough to see their aunt. A short distance away, Ethel stood surrounded by a circle of women from the Seniors Social Circle. She looked like a general issuing orders as the ladies nodded repeatedly in response to what-ever she was saying.

It saddened Alice that Louise and their aunt were not on speaking terms. As she watched, Ethel swept out of the sanctuary without a backward glance, and Alice saw Louise register the slight. Her shoulders slumped just for a moment before she regained her customary proper posture, but Alice knew she was hurt. Ethel regularly stopped and spoke with each of her nieces after church. She already had hugged Jane and bid Alice good-bye. To fail to greet Louise today made Ethel's pique as plain as if she had painted a sign saying that she still was angry with Louise.

"Alice?" She heard June call her name and looked toward her traveling companion. "Are you ready to go?"

Excitement swelled within her, sidetracking all other thought. "Just let me say good-bye to my sisters and then we'll be off."

Chapter Seven

W e're here! We're finally here!"

"I'm so excited." Alice looked around as June pulled the huge SUV into a lane where a sign welcomed them to Camp Compassion Monday afternoon. They had left Acorn Hill right after church Sunday and taken turns at the wheel every three hours, driving straight through the night.

Alice was stiff and creaky and tired of being in the car, but those feelings vanished as she looked forward to finally getting started.

There was a chain-link fence with a closed gate blocking their path. An enormous man in a T-shirt that bore the phrase, "I love my Chihuahua," with a heart symbol substituted for the second word, ambled toward them.

June rolled down her window. "Hello."

"Can I help you?" he asked in a Southern accent so heavy Alice wasn't sure she'd understood him at first.

"We're here to volunteer," said June, ruffling her short silver blonde hair and massaging her neck. Alice leaned across the console dividing the front seats and added. "Dr. Mark Graves is expecting us."

"Hey, come on in. We can always use more hands. I'm Kyle." The man's wide smile flashed in his dark face, revealing a gold front tooth.

"I'm June and this is Alice. We're happy to be here."

Kyle unlocked the gate and stood back to motion them through.

As they drove forward, June looked around. "Which way should I go, do you think?"

Alice pointed to the right, where a muddy track showed tire marks. "It looks like vehicles went this way." She rolled down her passenger window and smiled as a woman passed them and waved. "Could you please tell us where to park?"

The woman pointed with her free hand; the other had a firm grip on a leash against which a fat black Lab was straining. "If you're staying, we pitch our tents back there. If you have supplies, drive over to the little white house and ask for Joe."

June turned toward the house. "We need to drop off all these supplies first, because we can't even get to our tent until we do."

As the SUV rolled to a stop, Alice opened her door and stepped out. Going around to the rear of the vehicle, she opened the gate and surveyed the floor-to-ceiling stacks of boxes. "I hope you ate your Wheaties this morning."

June groaned, her slight shoulders slumping as she joined Alice. "I wonder if we can get some help with this stuff."

"Alice!" She barely had time to turn around before a man's arms swept her into a bear hug.

"Mark! For heaven's sake." She was laughing, but her heart gave a little skip at the sudden reunion.

"I'm so glad you made it. How was your trip?" Mark stepped back and smiled at her.

"Long," she said with a heartfelt sigh. "But we're here now. With your supplies," she added, hitching her thumb at the packed vehicle behind them. "Mark, you remember June Carter."

"Great to meet you." Mark shook June's hand. A tall man, he dwarfed Alice's traveling companion. "Let me find Riley and introduce you two. He is the supplies manager, and he will need to inventory all this stuff before I start grabbing it out of his hands. We need the antibiotics badly." Mark looked around, then cupped his hands to his mouth and yelled, "Riley! Job for you."

A young man in a red T-shirt with sleeves raggedly torn off at the shoulders appeared from around the corner of the house. In one ear he wore five silver earrings in different sizes. Both wrists were tattooed so heavily that he appeared to be wearing bracelets, and his hair was dark at the roots and colored a bold yellow blonde at the tips, cut short to spike straight out all over his head. "Yo, Doc. Whassup?"

Do not judge, Alice reminded herself. He's here, so he must be a good man. "Hello," she said, offering her hand. "I'm Alice and this is June. We've brought medical supplies for Mark—Dr. Graves—and some other things from our community."

Riley shook her hand enthusiastically. "Cool beans! Let me round up a few more hands and we'll get this stuff inside." He shook a stern finger at Mark. "And don't you be making off with any of it until I've had a chance to log it in."

"Wouldn't think of it," Mark assured him with a grin. As Riley sprinted away, Mark turned back to Alice and June. "Riley worked at a shelter that was destroyed in the storm. He single-handedly rescued seven dogs and nine cats whose cages were flooding. Some of the dogs in the lower cages had to swim in place before he could get to them. He put them all in his pickup and barely got out before the road washed away."

"I suspect we're going to hear many stories of miracle workers this week, aren't we?" Alice said.

Mark nodded, and she thought she saw the sheen of tears in his eyes for just a moment. "The selflessness of all these people who dropped everything in their daily lives and came to help is overwhelming. Every single one of them—you included—is a miracle in my eyes."

"We haven't done anything yet." Alice smiled to lighten the mood.

"Joe." Mark beckoned to another man who was hustling by with a clipboard in one hand and a walkie-talkie in the other. "This is Alice, and this is June. They're friends from home, here to work for a few days."

"Great!" Joe shook Alice's hand with an enthusiastic grip so firm she winced. Then he produced a pen. "Write down your names and addresses for me, the dates you'll be here, and what expertise you may have."

"I don't work with animals on a regular basis," Alice confessed as she took the clipboard and began to write.

"She's a nurse," Mark said at almost the same moment.

"A nurse. Fantastic. We don't just need animal-care workers, although we love them." Joe motioned to the front door of the house. "If you wouldn't mind, there's a girl inside with a pretty ugly cut across her palm that you might take a look at. She doesn't want to go to the medical center, but I think she should."

"I'd be glad to check on her."

Alice turned, but Joe grasped her elbow. "It's been cleaned and bandaged. It's not urgent. I'd just like to know if she's going to need stitches."

"I work with cats," June told him, "but I can help with other things too."

"Do you do laundry?" Joe looked sheepish. "It's not a glamorous job, but it's desperately needed. We're running out of towels again. It's near the cat room," he added with a hopeful expression. "You could work in there between loads."

"Lead on," June said. "I don't mind a bit."

"You're a saint." Joe turned to Mark. "You busy?"

"Not right this second."

"Want to give them the two-minute tour before they get started?"

"With pleasure. Let's help Riley unload this stuff first."

With the help of Mark, Riley and two female volunteers he'd rounded up, Alice and June got all the supplies they'd brought unloaded in a few minutes. Then Mark hopped into the SUV and took them quickly around the camp.

In the tiny house was the critical care unit, where very sick dogs were taken; the cat room; a room for exotics and birds; the laundry room; and the office, where supplies were kept. Outside the house was a canopy under which were several lawn chairs for people taking breaks. A tractor-trailer bed parked beside the house held pallets stacked with dry pet food, blankets, towels and kitty litter. Cat pans and dog kennels were stored beneath it in orderly fashion, arranged by size. There was another canopied area under which were baby pools for bathing incoming animals, pools of bleach water for sterilizing bowls and kennels, and a table full of every kind of pet shampoo imaginable.

Next they walked a path through a mountain of supplies. Two women were separating the food, blankets and towels, leashes, collars and other items into groups, and several other people were carrying them back to the tractor-trailer for storage.

Farther along the track were long lines of chain-link dog kennels, nearly all full. Canopies above them provided shade, Alice was glad to see. Some held several dogs, and Mark explained that as they got to know the animals, the ones that were not aggressive were housed together to make room for newcomers. A dog-walking area was roped off with bright yellow rope, and a large area surrounded by chain-link fencing was available for exercising dogs with balls and Frisbees.

At the very back of the extensive setup were the "accommodations." Tents, picnic canopies, a few campers and one enormous RV filled the space. Behind the house, just a short walk from the tent area, were two portable toilets and an enclosed area that Mark explained was partitioned into a primitive shower. Water was at a premium, so people were asked not to use the shower more than once every couple of days.

Alice and June exchanged wry glances. "I'm glad we were forewarned, or we might be having heart palpitations right about now," June said.

"So that's everything," Mark said. "Let's set up your tent. You probably won't get back here again until bedtime, and by then you'll be awfully glad you did."

With Mark's help, they got June's tent pitched quickly, their air mattresses inflated and their sleeping bags unrolled. June hung a lantern from the center of the tent and set up two camp chairs and a tray table. Since June owned so much equipment, they hadn't needed to borrow Shelby's things after all. "There. Home sweet home."

"Almost." Alice went to the SUV and rummaged in her bag for a moment. Returning to the tent, she laid her Bible on the table. "There."

Mark nodded. "An excellent touch. I brought mine as well. Sorry to rush off, but I need to get back to the house." He ducked out of the tent.

"Wait for me. I need to look at that girl's hand," Alice said.

"And I have laundry and kitties waiting." June started off along the path toward the front of the lot where the house stood.

"Bring a flashlight," Mark said to Alice as they prepared to follow June. "It gets dark quickly, and that path is rough when you can't see where you're walking."

Alice immediately headed for the house. The young woman of whom Joe had spoken lay on a sofa in the office, which consisted mostly of a small desk, two sofas and a table surrounded by piles and piles of pet medications.

"Hi, I'm Alice," she said to her patient.

"I'm Frannie." The young woman held up her roughly bandaged hand. "And this is the result of my losing battle with a bale of wire."

"Ouch!" Alice winced as she began to unwrap the wound. "Let's just take a quick look at this."

"I don't want to go to the hospital," Frannie said quickly. "It'll take too much time away from my work here."

"Which you're going to miss anyway if this gets infected," Alice pointed out. She pulled away the gauze and inspected the cut that stretched across the young woman's palm. "I really think you should get this stitched up. I can put some butterfly bandages on it to hold the edges together for now, but you need to see a doctor."

Frannie sighed. "I knew you were going to say that. Can't you just stitch it up?"

Alice shook her head. "Not without a doctor seeing you. And you probably need a tetanus shot as well."

After another volunteer drove Frannie off to the nearest emergency clinic, Alice cleaned and bandaged a succession of minor injuries. She monitored one young woman who'd had an asthma attack and sent someone back to the tents for the girl's inhaler.

In between nursing people, she helped in the canine critical care unit. Mark took one small dog with a large wound on its belly to the mobile vet clinic, leaving in charge one of the two veterinary technicians who had come along with him.

Gina was dark-skinned with enormous brown eyes and a smile that lit up the room. "I'm afraid your nursing talents may be wasted here," she told Alice with a grin. "Mostly, we clean up messes, give medications and check vitals."

Alice smiled back. "And just what do you think nurses do?"

Gina laughed. "You have a point."

"So where shall I begin?"

"You could start taking the dogs out for their late walks. Be sure you don't bring them back in until they've relieved themselves. Plastic bags are on the table you'll pass at the entrance to the dog-walk area, and there are garbage cans for the waste. Several water stations are set up around the camp."

"All right." Alice hesitated. "I'm willing but not particularly knowledgeable. Could you show me how to get a dog out of its cage? After all, they don't know me from Adam. Will they bite?"

"That's unlikely. However, I can't promise you it will never happen. Over here is a poster with canine postures and expressions on it. You usually can tell when one is scared as opposed to aggressive. The important thing to remember is to move slowly and speak gently. We don't want to scare them any more than they are already." Gina took a leash down from a hook on the wall and demonstrated the correct way of using it by slipping the lead onto Alice's wrist. Then she let Alice try it on her. "I'll get the first dog out for you."

Gina released the latch on a cage and put the slip lead on the first dog, which she said was a beagle mix, probably still less than a year old. Then she lifted the dog down from the waist-high kennel, and Alice could see its ribs and hip-bones. "A lot of these guys have been starved and their energy's pretty low. They may not be able to jump in and out of the higher kennels."

Alice nodded as she accepted the lead. "Okay, little man. I'm going to take good care of you." She let the puppy sniff her hand, then gently petted it before leading it out the door and into the exercise area.

∽

It was nine o'clock on their first night at Camp Compassion, and Alice felt as if she had been there for days already. She'd met at least a dozen people.

Now, as Alice and June stumbled along the path behind the beam of their flashlight, June sighed. "I'm hungry, but I might be too tired to eat."

"Me too." Alice put a hand to the small of her back and rubbed at the sore muscles. "I thought I was in reasonably good shape until we arrived here."

June laughed. "I feel the same way. Guess we've been proven wrong."

Back at the tent, the two women opened bottles of water and prepackaged meals, which they heated over a small Coleman stove while they washed up with baby wipes. After eating, they rolled down the window flaps and fastened the zipper door from the inside, then doused the lantern and changed out of their filthy clothing.

"Put your things in a trash bag and I'll wash them while I'm doing towels tomorrow," June suggested. "Good night."

"Good night." Alice lay down with a grateful sigh on her air mattress as June did the same.

"Lord," said Alice quietly, "thank You for bringing us safely to this camp. Thank You for all these amazing people around us, for moving our hearts and spirits to care for Your creatures. Guide our hands to comfort and to heal. Give us renewed strength when we tire. We thank You for the many blessings You have bestowed on us. In the name of Your Son, our Lord Jesus Christ. Amen."

She turned on her side...and slept.

Chapter Eight

Alice's second day at Camp Compassion began just as the sky was growing light. The dogs, which had been quiet throughout the night, began to bark and pace as soon as they saw the first person walking through camp.

Alice staggered to her feet, unzipped the tent and stepped out into the fresh, cool air.

"Good morning!" At a pop-up camper next to the spot Alice and June's tent was pitched, a dark-haired woman stood, twisting a single long braid up into an efficient bun atop her head. She was taller than Alice's five-foot-six-inch height and strongly built. She stepped closer and extended a hand.

"Good morning."

"I'm Ellen."

"I'm Alice. My friend June and I just arrived yesterday."

The woman gestured to her camper, from which the sounds of other people stirring could be heard. "My children and I have been here for three days. We're from Chicago."

"We're from southern Pennsylvania, not far from Philadelphia. Is there anything we should do first, or do we just look for jobs that need to be done?"

"There are volunteers assigned to feeding and walking this morning. Afterward, we'll all gather for the daily camp meeting. Where were you working yesterday?"

"I was in the critical care unit. June was doing laundry and helping with cats."

"That's where you probably should go if you're ready to get to work. Ah, here they are." Ellen grinned as two teenagers with dark, curly hair emerged from the camper. Both were tall, although the girl was built more delicately than either her mother or her strapping brother. "Royce, Miranda, this is Alice."

"Hello, Alice," they said in unison. Then they looked at each other and laughed. "You owe me a Coke," said Miranda.

As tall as she was, her brother still topped her by several inches, but their resemblance was striking. "We're twins," she said when she saw Alice studying them. "We love animals and we thought this would be a cool thing to do."

"Me too. But how did you get out of school?" Alice asked.

The boy said, "We're high school seniors. We've already taken our SATs and submitted college applications—"

"So Mom thought we could afford to miss a week of school," his sister finished.

"The principal didn't have a problem with it," Ellen told Alice. "He thought it would be a great learning experience."

As the twins turned away to grab a bite of breakfast pastries, Alice said, "I can't imagine how this experience would have affected me at their age. I might have wound up in animal care instead of nursing."

"I know what you mean. I'm a legal secretary. But I swear to you, if I didn't have two kids to support, I'd quit and go back to school to become a veterinary technician. I've been happy to pitch in, but I keep thinking I could be so much more useful if I knew more about treating animals."

"I don't know much either. I spent most of yesterday helping in the CCU, cleaning kennels and feeding. I didn't mind though. Someone has to do it."

"And there are plenty of us to share the load," Miranda said. "I think it's amazingly cool that all these people came down here to help." She gestured around them.

"It is, indeed." Alice turned to duck back into her tent. "It's lovely to meet all of you. I'm sure I'll see you again later."

"Who was that?" June was just crawling out of her sleeping bag.

"Our next-door neighbors. A mom with two high school students. They're from Chicago."

"The lady in charge of the cat room is from Montana."

"Montana! That makes me feel as if we didn't have a long trip at all."

June paused in the act of shaking out her sleeping bag. "I wonder what we should do this morning."

"Ellen from next door said to do the same thing you did yesterday. There is a camp meeting every morning and I suppose assignments are given there."

The two women tidied up their tent and ate boxes of raisins and donuts they had purchased before they left what Alice thought of as "civilization." Then they walked up to the little white house that served as the center of operations. Alice headed for the CCU while June went to start yet another load of soiled towels and begin feeding cats.

"Good morning, Alice." Gina, the perky, pretty vet tech with whom Alice had enjoyed working the day before, already was hard at work.

"Good morning. What would you like me to do?"

Gina gestured to a bank of kennels along the far wall. "Start walking those guys, especially the ones whose cages are still clean and dry. I'll clean out each kennel while you're outside."

Alice reached for a slip lead. The first dog she took out was a young white pit bull. He sat in the back corner of his cage eyeing her mournfully. Alice said a quick prayer for safety and took a deep breath. "Hi, baby boy. Remember me? I'm your friend Alice and I'm going to take you outside now." She moved toward the dog, slipped the lead over his head and took in the slack. The dog slowly rose to his feet and came listlessly to the door of the kennel, where Alice lifted him down. He promptly leaned against her legs. He was so thin she could see every rib along his side. "You're going to feel better soon," she promised him, stroking his broad head. "A day or so of good meals and you'll get your bounce back."

An hour later, all the dogs had been cared for.

"Good work, Alice," Gina said. "You're a natural with these dogs."

"They're just patients in need," Alice said, embarrassed by the praise.

"Mark tells me you two have known each other a long time." Gina's knowing smile made Alice chuckle.

"We've been friends since college." She emphasized the *friends* part. "How do you know him?"

"I work for a veterinary dental specialist who cares for the zoo's animals occasionally. I knew Mark slightly, and when I heard he was going to bring a clinic down, I jumped at the chance to come along." Gina checked her watch. "We'd better get outside. There's a staff meeting in front of the cleaning canopy at nine."

More than two dozen people were milling around near the canopy where the bowls and kennels were cleaned. Alice spotted June chatting with the twins' mother Ellen, and moved through the group to their side just as Joe climbed atop a sturdy wooden box and began to speak.

"Good morning, people. It's another beautiful autumn day and we've got a lot to do: dogs to walk, cats to cuddle, friends to make." He had such a surfeit of energy that a ripple of laughter ran through the crowd. "We have two new faces in the crowd this morning. Alice and June from Pennsylvania, raise your hands."

The two women smiled and raised their hands in a wave at those around them.

"Don't forget your name tags, everyone. Hanna's hand-ing them around." Joe said, gesturing at a short brunette going from person to person with a marker. Each person wrote his or her name on a sticky tag, which was plastered to the front of his or her T-shirt.

Joe glanced down at his clipboard, which Alice was beginning to suspect he clutched in one hand even while sleeping. "Today we say farewell to the Brinkleys. What time are you guys taking off?"

"As soon as the meeting's over," said a burly man in overalls and a wide straw hat. The woman beside him had tears running down her cheeks.

"You know we don't want to go," she said, "but our grandkids are taking care of our own animals while we're down here, and we can't ask them to stay any longer. As it is, they won't let us pay them."

"Please extend our thanks to them for freeing you to join us," Joe said. "You two have been fantastic." He consulted his clipboard. "Let's start with housekeeping business. A rottweiler rescue group from New Jersey is coming today. They're taking the two males with yellow tags in the main kennels. There also are two male rotties with red tags. Those are owned and may not be moved from this site. Their owners are being contacted. Let's not have any mixups, folks. There's also a shelter in Tennessee sending down an air-conditioned RV with ten kennels in it. They'll take some of the dogs and a few cats back with them."

Joe cleared his throat. "We had no intake last night because we were too full. But now that we have a few vacancies, the teams will go out today, and we'll be working tonight. We also have a new vet arriving so there will be two stations. And there's a groomer coming by today to shave down that big red chow. Maybe it will improve her disposition. The dog's, not the groomer's," he added as people chuckled. "Any questions or comments?"

A redheaded woman near the back raised a hand. "Joe, please remind people to be sure the lids are on the garbage cans tightly. I know summer's over, but it's awfully warm. There are still flies, which mean maggots."

"Good reminder. Anything else?"

Gina spoke up. "Joe, the air-conditioning in the critical care unit does not seem to be cooling very well."

Joe pointed at a lean, balding man. "See Shel."

"Shel is our fix-it king," Gina murmured to Alice. "He can repair anything."

Joe pointed to Hanna again after a short silence. "That's it, people. See Hanna for daily assignments and be sure you know what station you'll be manning this evening. Keep up the good work."

As the crowd dispersed, Alice joined the group around Hanna. "Kennel cleaning: Foster and Aidan. Clean team: Edith, Jacqui and Mike. Cat room: Jules and June. June, are you still helping with laundry?"

"I sure am," said June.

"Thanks."

"Do you have an assignment for me?" Alice asked.

Hanna consulted her list. "Alice, right?"

"Yes, from Pennsylvania."

The girl laughed. She was probably in her early twenties, but she looked much younger. Damp ringlets of shining brown hair curling around her face framed her wide blue eyes and sweet smile. "Alice from Pennsylvania…let's see. Oh, here you are. Mark and Gina want you in CCU again today, and Joe would like you to be on call for any human medical problems."

"Thank you. Where are you from?"

"Nowhere. I mean, I'm from right here. I'm the executive director of this humane society, the Gulf Coast Animal Protection Team. When Riley lost his building, I invited him to bring his animals here. He kept going back to rescue others, and word got around that we were taking animals. Things got crazy around here. I realized we couldn't handle an operation this big, so I called HOUS for national assistance. That's when Joe came in."

"I see. That was wise of you."

Hanna smiled wryly. "It was self-protection. I was totally overwhelmed. The place was a madhouse. Joe, with his gift for organization, was a gift from heaven."

Alice smiled. "I've seen a lot of those around here since I arrived."

Hanna nodded her head. "So have I.

⸙

That evening, Ellen invited Alice and June to have dinner with the twins and her.

Alice had three bananas and June brought cookies, and fruit juice in single-serving boxes. To their surprise,

Ellen had two box mixes of noodles with Alfredo sauce, which she managed to cook for thirty minutes on a Coleman stove a great deal more sophisticated than June's.

"This was an excellent meal," Alice said. "Thank you so much for inviting us."

"Teenagers," Ellen said. "I know they require a lot of fuel, so I stocked up on anything I thought I could manage to cook on this stove."

"You're certainly more adventurous than I am." June tore open the package of cookies. "I'm happy if I can boil water for rice or instant oatmeal on mine."

Ellen chuckled. "I'll have to teach you some of my tricks while we're here."

"Mom can do amazing things with a camp stove," Miranda chimed in.

"So tell us about yourselves," Alice said to the twins. "You said you have applied to colleges, but you didn't mention where."

"I just received my acceptance to the University of Michigan," Miranda said promptly. "And Royce already has been accepted at schools in Florida and Massachusetts. He wants to be a marine biologist."

"And you?" Alice had already learned that Miranda did most of the talking for the pair. Royce was pleasant, courteous and seemed quite happy to sit back and let his sister occupy the limelight.

"Music," Miranda said. "I sing and play French horn. I don't know if I want to teach or perform, but I know I want to continue music studies."

"*INCOMING!*" The voice was Joe's, amplified by a bullhorn. "I need everybody at the staging area in five minutes."

"Let's go, Royce." Miranda scrambled to her feet as Ellen hastily cleaned up the remains of the meal. "I heard they were going to search a new area today, so we probably are going to get a lot of animals tonight. The number of rescues has been tapering off recently," Miranda told June and Alice, "but if the new area hasn't been scouted yet, it's possible they have found pets alive." She and Royce stomped their feet into rubber barn boots and took off along the path. All around the camping area, flashlights and lanterns bobbed wildly as people rushed to get to their stations.

Alice had been assigned a job, as had June, and each rushed to find her team leader. Alice's team leader was Corinne, the kennel manager. As the dogs were unloaded, Corinne and a dog trainer assessed each one.

"Most of them are docile," said Corinne to the assembled volunteers. "They're starved and weak and scared to death, very dispirited. Occasionally we get a dog that is not very happy, and we do not expect you to handle any of the dangerous ones. That's our job."

Alice was a bit relieved. She had not fully realized the extent of the work to be done when she first envisioned volunteering, and seeing all the required skills made her feel somewhat inadequate.

She stood back as the first set of kennels was unloaded from a truck. The men handling the crates were Darrell and Oren, and Alice learned that both men were locals. They were donating the use of their vehicles and their time to locate animals.

"They started doing this the second day Riley went out, and they've been at it ever since," Miranda told her. "They're like superheroes or something."

Royce took the first dog, a black Lab so weak he could not even walk on his own. Alice's eyes teared as Royce scooped up the animal and headed for the bathing area.

Miranda went next, getting a beagle whose tail feebly wagged as it was handed out of its kennel wrapped in a blanket. "Leg injury," said Corinne. "Skip the bath. Take this one directly to the intake station and then give it vet priority."

Two more dogs were unloaded: a pit bull, who was able to walk on his own, although Alice could count each of his ribs; and a huge rottweiler that required two men to carry it on a blanket. Kyle, the front-gate guard, and tattooed Riley stepped forward.

"Careful," Corinne warned. "She's pregnant. Due pretty soon and not looking too good." As the men lifted the blanket, the rottie lifted her massive head for a moment, then let it flop back down as if she was too ill to care what was happening.

Oren drove the first pickup truck away and Darrell backed a second one into the unloading zone.

"Stand back," Corinne said as she opened the back of the truck and shone a flashlight on the first dog. Alice could hear a steady rumbling growl interspersed with the occasional snarl or bark. "This one's going to take some finesse." Corinne took a stick with an expandable piece on the end and stuck it through the cage bars. Once it was inside, she released a trigger, and the end of the stick became a wide restraint that she pressed against the dog.

The dog went wild at first, biting at the stick and turning flips in the confined space. Finally, when it appeared to have exhausted its energy, it stood panting in the back of the cage with the restraint pressed against its chest.

"Go around to the side and say something to it," Corinne instructed another volunteer.

"What do I say?"

"Anything. We just need to distract him for a moment."

The dog handler, Lucinda, held a long pole with a loop on it. As another volunteer cautiously opened the kennel door a scant inch, Lucinda maneuvered her pole through. The dog snarled at her until the volunteer stepped into its side view and spoke to it. Startled, the dog turned to snap futilely at the speaker. Lucinda seized the opportunity to neatly slip the loop over the dog's head and tighten it.

"This is hard to watch," said a man behind Alice. "But it's the safest way to handle him. He's probably just frightened. He doesn't know we want to make his life better. A lot of these scary ones become different animals after a few meals and a couple days of kindness."

Lucinda tugged and the dog rushed forward, banging open the cage door. He whirled and tried to bite the catchpole, but Lucinda took off at a smart clip, expertly holding the dog at a distance. Finally, the dog stopped resisting. He began to trot along beside Lucinda, ignoring the pole.

"All right." Corinne mimed wiping sweat from her brow. "Let's hope he's the only one with enough energy to be feisty tonight." She peered into the next kennel, then opened the door and reached in. Over her shoulder, she said, "Alice, this is a good one for you to start with."

As Corinne lifted a small, dark-colored cocker spaniel from its kennel and stood it on its feet, Alice stepped forward. Corinne handed her the purple slip lead she had placed on the dog and looped a piece of elastic with an index card encased in plastic around Alice's wrist. "Whatever you do, do not lose this information. Give it to the people at the intake table." She looked down at the dog. "I believe this one can walk on its own. If not, just ask for help if you're nervous at all about picking it up."

"Hi, baby." Alice knelt and extended a fisted hand as she had seen the others do. The cocker did not even try to sniff her, just stood there with its head hanging down. "Come on, sweetheart, we're going to get you feeling better. Let's go this way."

The little dog walked docilely behind her as she coaxed it over to the bathing station, where a group of people waited.

"What a pretty little one," said Ellen. She wore elbow-length rubber gloves, and she scooped up the dog, setting it in a baby pool filled with a soapy mix. "A lot of them have been soaked in oil or other gunk," she told Alice as she poured shampoo over the cocker and quickly went over its body. To Alice's surprise, the newly cleaned dog was black and white. "We clean them up and then they get a flea dip. After that, you take her over to that table, where Hanna will do her paperwork."

Alice spoke softly to the little dog as it was rinsed and then sent into the flea dip. Wet, it was apparent that the dog had not eaten in a long time. Like many of the others she had seen, it was emaciated to the point of looking skeletal. After a quick towel dry, a volunteer laid a small towel over the dog's back like a blanket. "Okay, off you go."

At the intake table, Alice's dog received a collar with a number on it. She surrendered the index card, and its information was transferred to the dog's record with the same number. The dog was weighed and listed as a female black-and-white parti-color cocker spaniel.

Next, a vet examined the dog. To Alice's disappointment, her dog had not been placed in Mark's line, but in that of the vet who had just arrived that afternoon. She was watching Mark, at the next table, go over the pregnant rottweiler when a grouchy voice said, "Hey, lady. Quit wasting my time and get that dog on the table."

Gina, her friend from the CCU, was the vet tech assisting, and she rolled her eyes as Alice lifted the cocker onto the exam table. The vet's name tag said Dr. Spade. Alice was slightly surprised. All the other folks around camp, from vets to volunteers, wrote their first names on their own name tags.

Dr. Spade completely ignored her while he examined the cocker, addressing his comments to Gina. As the vet tech laid the little dog on its side, Alice heard Gina suck in her breath.

"What's wrong?"

Dr. Spade did not appear to have heard her. Gina said, "Tumor." She had her hands full as the cocker spaniel began to struggle and growl.

Alice hurried around the head of the table and knelt, looking into the dog's eyes. "It's all right, girl. You're going to be all right."

The dog quieted. Gina said, "Wow, she likes you."

"Excuse me." The vet's voice was sarcastic and cutting. He practically pushed Alice out of the way. As he examined the tumor, the dog became more and more agitated. Finally, the vet was done, and Gina set the dog on the ground.

The cocker rushed to Alice's side and cowered against her legs. Gina's eyebrows went up and her eyes twinkled. "Looks like you've got a new friend."

"Don't get too attached," Dr. Spade said brusquely. "That tumor looks malignant. If it's metastasized, she won't make it. Better put her in the CCU where we can see how she does."

Alice was indignant, but she bit her tongue and led her small charge away. Don't get too attached, indeed. She did not care if the dog had one day or ten years left to live, the animal deserved as much love as anyone could give until an owner was found or it was taken into foster care. After placing the cocker in a kennel in critical care with water and a small amount of food, Alice returned to the unloading zone.

Twice more, she shepherded dogs through the intake process. Her second charge was a puppy with a deep wound on its throat. The puppy was so docile and quiet she feared it had other injuries, but when Mark examined the pup, he did not think the wound was as serious as Alice thought. He bet her a cookie that the puppy would be on its feet with its tail wagging by the following evening.

"I hope so." She felt her lip tremble.

Mark put an arm around her shoulders and hugged her briefly. "You're doing a great job. It's been a long day."

Alice allowed herself to rest her head against Mark's shoulder for a moment, leaning on his strength. "There are only a few dogs left to be examined," she told him. "I'm almost done."

Her next dog was a tiny Yorkie who smelled so bad that she had to breathe through her mouth as she carried him to the bathing area. The index card said that it had been found in a sewer pipe, and Alice had no trouble believing this. Even so, the terrier was livelier than most of the other dogs brought in. It yapped and tried to lick Alice's face after its bath, when she finally could stand to get close to it. When the dog was weighed, the scale did not even reach four pounds, and everyone laughed.

"He's a little loud mouth," said Hanna as she went through his paperwork.

Unlike Alice's first two dogs, the male Yorkie was healthy and did not need to go into the CCU, although he was placed in a special area designated for what one volunteer affectionately called "the pocket pups."

It was past eleven by the time Alice went looking for June for their walk back to the tent. As she'd suspected, she found her friend in the cat room. After waiting a few minutes for June to bottle-feed an orphaned kitten, the two women headed for their tent.

Alice shared her evening's work with June. As they washed up, her companion told Alice about the seven cats that had been brought in. "One of the people on the search team told me she expects they'll be finding more cats in the next few weeks. She said that the cats are just now starting to get hungry enough to come out from their hiding places when the rescue teams arrive."

"It breaks my heart to think about how all the animals must feel, wondering where their families have gone. Imagine how afraid they must be."

June reached up to turn out the lantern as Alice crawled onto her air mattress. "I know. But think of the ones we helped tonight. In a few days they'll be feeling better, and perhaps some of them can be reunited with their families."

Chapter Nine

Jane was raking leaves onto a sheet of plastic in the yard Wednesday morning. She already had had a busy day, rising early to get a six thirty breakfast on the table for a pair of sisters who were traveling home to Maine for Thanksgiving. The women had stayed only the one night, but they were delightfully enthusiastic about the inn and expressed a desire to return one day. Jane silently congratulated herself on her menu, whole-wheat French toast stuffed with cream cheese and pecans, coated with cinnamon-butter sauce and topped with a light dusting of powdered sugar.

She was just about to drag off her leaves to the back when Lloyd Tynan came driving by. In the passenger seat, Jane could see her aunt. Lloyd turned into the driveway as Jane waved and leaned on her rake. The car continued on to the parking area at the back of the house, and by the time Jane walked to meet them, Lloyd had turned around and dropped off Ethel. She and Jane met outside the back door, and both waved good-bye to Lloyd.

"Hello, Aunt Ethel. Please come in. Would you like some coffee or tea? And I just made banana cream pie this morning. You'll have to let me know if it tastes all right."

Ethel followed Jane into the kitchen, stopping to remove her coat and hang it on a hook near the door. "Thank you, dear. I would love a cup of tea. I'm sure your banana cream pie does not need my seal of approval, but I'll be happy to give it anyway."

Jane chuckled. "Thank you." She busied herself preparing the snack.

"I stopped to tell you about last night's board meeting," Ethel announced.

"Oh, I forgot there was a meeting. I'll have to remember this so I can tell Alice about it when she calls."

"Tell her I am remembering her in my prayers and that I expect her to be very careful down there."

"I will." Jane brought tea and pie to the table and sank into a seat at an angle to her aunt's. "So what happened at the board meeting?" She propped her chin on her hand and prepared for one of Ethel's lengthy stories.

She wasn't disappointed.

"Well." Ethel took a dainty sip of her drink. "Alice wasn't there, of course, or June. So our attendance was down. Lloyd and me, Fred, Pastor Henry and Patsy, Cyril and…who am I forgetting? Rev. Thompson had another meeting. Oh, Sylvia. And Florence." She sniffed. "I believe she thinks that there won't be any decent crafts to sell except for those she personally oversees."

Jane choked back a laugh. Diplomatically, she said, "We'll have plenty of lovely things from your Seniors Social Circle. They have planned a surprising number of donations. Although I am grateful for the way Florence has embraced the project."

"Yes. Well, maybe next year she'll be a little more supportive from the get-go. It's always easier to jump on the bandwagon once it's underway."

"So what else have you decided to do?" Jane knew from experience that the only thing to do when her aunt got on the topic of her differences with Florence Simpson was to distract Ethel.

"I had another idea." Ethel sat forward. "We had intended to use the Assembly Room, but I want to put up a canopy or tent outside."

"A canopy?" Jane remembered Louise saying something about Ethel's plan to move the entire crafts fair outside. "For what?"

"Some of the crafters with weatherproof items can have booth space out there. It'll give us more revenue. And I thought it might be nice to have hot chocolate and cider for sale, maybe some demonstrations of traditional crafts and equipment."

Jane couldn't think of anything that fit into that category offhand. "Such as?"

"A cider press," Ethel said. "A spinning wheel. Or even sheep shearing. Things like that."

Jane raised her eyebrows. "Sounds like fun, if you can get all that organized in—" She glanced at the calendar. "Three and a half weeks."

"Oh, I've already made some calls. Why don't you tell me what you've been doing?"

Jane stretched across the table for the list she had been working with earlier that morning. She reeled off the names of people who had agreed to make crafts to benefit the church. Next, she listed the vendors who had committed to purchase space at the fair.

"Goodness!" Ethel was beaming. "You've been a busy woman, Jane. Have you—"

"Jane, I can't find the—" Louise came walking briskly into the kitchen. When she saw Ethel, she stopped.

Ethel seemed just as taken aback. Then, right before Jane's eyes, her aunt set down her teacup and rose. "Well, Jane, I must be getting on my way. I really only stopped to tell you about the board meeting and get an update." She rose and majestically sailed out the door, gathering up her coat on the way.

Jane was too shocked to speak. Their aunt was just… just *impossible* sometimes.

"Did you see that? How unreasonable can a person be? She didn't even acknowledge my presence." Louise's tone underscored her disappointment.

"Oh, Louise, I'm sure Aunt Ethel didn't mean—"

"Yes, she did. That was a direct cut. Just the way those women in Atlanta treated Scarlett O'Hara in *Gone with the Wind*."

Scarlett O'Hara? Jane could not picture Louise relating to the heroine of a romantic fiction epic like Margaret Mitchell's beloved story. "She doesn't know what to say to you," she told her. "I suspect she feels guilty."

"Well, she need not bother." Louise raised her chin in a manner that Jane thought absolutely defined her eldest sister's personality. "I do not intend to let it matter. And I hope you will convey to her that it didn't."

"Ho now! Don't put me in the middle of this." Jane got up and walked to the counter. "How about a piece of banana cream pie? It's guaranteed to make you feel better." She decided not to mention that Ethel also had enjoyed it.

Wednesday afternoon, Alice was in the CCU checking on the four-legged patients. Many of the dogs who had come in were gone already, either taken by a rescue group or moved to the outside runs as their health improved. She stroked the head of the sweet rottweiler. They would not move her anywhere in her advanced state of pregnancy. Some of the volunteers had started a pool on when and how many pups would be born.

Then she checked on the dog about whom she was most concerned, a German shepherd that had been brought in last night. According to Darrell and Oren, the dog had been found lying on a broken board beneath a collapsed house. They only found it because a window of the house bore a sticker that said, "In case of fire, there are x number of pets inside." Oren demanded Darrell stop so he could take a quick look. The dog, a large male, did not protest at all when they moved him. Mark put in an intravenous line to rehydrate the dog and balance its electrolytes, but the animal had yet to take a drink or eat a single thing. Alice stayed with him awhile, stroking his fur and talking softly to him.

Finally, she took her cocker spaniel outside. The little girl quickly had made a place in Alice's heart for herself. Despite the large tumor attached to her belly, she trotted happily to the grassy area, then walked nicely at Alice's side until it was time to return her.

Walking through the carport with its rows of kennels stacked on each side, Alice opened the door and entered the cool, calm environment of the CCU. She opened the kennel door and bent to slip off the lead she had placed around the dog's neck.

"Don't put yourself in a position for that dog to bite you in the face," Dr. Spade ordered from the far side of the room.

Alice had not seen him because he was hidden by a bank of kennels. She pressed her lips together and urged the little dog back into her kennel gently. It was not in Alice's nature to respond sharply, but she was tempted during this unpleasant encounter.

The man had no social skills whatsoever. Already this morning, he had made one volunteer cry and ordered another one out of the CCU after the young man accidentally fed a dog the wrong kind of food. Alice was pretty sure the dog would not expire from eating one meal of a different type. Dr. Spade certainly hadn't needed to be so harsh.

Knowing that her further assistance would be rejected by the curt veterinarian, she left the CCU. Outside, there was a huge backlog of dog bowls to be washed, so she took a seat on a folding chair beneath one canopy. "Would you like some help?" she asked Edith. Edith was the oldest volunteer who had arrived to date. She claimed to be seventy-eight, although she was nearly as agile as Alice herself.

"I'd love it. Seems like every dog dish in the place is in that pile over there." Edith pointed to a nearby table.

"Better put on some gloves. That bleach will take the skin off your hands."

Alice chatted with Edith as they placed bowls in the baby pool filled with bleach, then scrubbed them and dropped them into a second pool of rinse water, where another helper fished them out and laid them in the sun to dry. Miranda, Alice's seventeen-year-old neighbor from the tents, ran back and forth delivering clean bowls and returning with more to be washed.

Alice and Edith were contentedly scrubbing away when a piercing scream tore through the air. Alice flinched, her eyes going to the source of the scream. It came from a young woman standing near the house. She was looking up and pointing. Alice took it in during one frozen split second. Her gaze lifted to the roof—just in time to see someone slide over the edge and fall to the ground.

Alice leaped to her feet. It seemed as if the entire camp was converging on the scene, but as she neared, several people cleared the way for her as they remembered she had medical training.

The person had fallen into a sizable, overgrown shrub and could not be seen. Alice dropped to her stomach and began to wiggle beneath the low-hanging branches when she felt a hand grab her ankle, preventing her from moving any farther.

"Just wait a minute there. Do not touch that person!" Alice recognized the voice of Dr. Spade.

Then she heard another voice. "Please take your hands off that woman. She is our acting medical professional." That was Joe. Still, the vise around her ankle didn't yield.

"Dr. Spade." The voice belonged to Mark. "Alice is a nurse. Please release her. Now!"

Alice had never in her entire life heard Mark sound so stern. He was one of the most even-tempered, gentle, kind people she had ever met. Those were some of the things that had attracted her to him so many years ago.

The pressure on her ankle disappeared. Alice began to squirm forward again. She could see a glimpse of blue T-shirt. Her heart sank as she saw how still the person lay.

"Hello," she said. "It's Alice, the nurse. Can you tell me what hurts?"

There was no response. As she neared, she realized the person was Riley, the tough-looking, tattooed young man in charge of supplies she had met when she first arrived. Since then, she had noticed how lively and cheerful Riley was. He seemed to be the self-appointed morale officer for the whole camp.

"Riley," she said as she reached him. "Can you hear me?" She took his wrist in her fingers, relieved to feel a strong, steady pulse. She leaned over him to check his pupils and started in surprise as he opened his eyes.

"Aw, man," he said slowly. "I hurt."

"I imagine you do. Can you tell me your full name?"

"Richard Rochester Riley III."

Alice took a moment to absorb the folly of parents who would give a child a name like that.

"Good, Riley. Where does it hurt?"

"Everywhere." He attempted a grin. "Tell me I was graceful. At least tell me I fell off that stupid roof like I knew what I was doing."

"I certainly hope you didn't." Alice couldn't help laughing at his comical words. "Now, what hurts the worst?"

"My head. My arm—ow!"

It was easy to see why he had yelled. Riley's forearm lay splayed at an awkward angle. "Don't move," she said. "Let me look you over. Where else does it hurt?"

She checked around his head but did not see any blood, and she was encouraged by how alert he seemed. There was no blood visible anywhere else either, although she would not know until he was moved.

"I think my arm is the only bad thing," Riley informed her. "I can feel my toes wiggling and my legs move. My back hurts a little, but I guess that's what happens when you take a header off a roof."

"I saw you fall," Alice said, "and it's lucky that you didn't really take a header. You just slid right off the edge on your back. The bush cushioned your fall somewhat. Stay still for a moment while I tell the others, all right?"

"Will do." Riley made an effort to smile, although she could see that he was in pain.

Alice backed out from beneath the bush as fast as she could. She didn't even want to think about what she looked like with her bottom in the air in front of an entire crowd of people, but it couldn't be helped. She was barely clear of the branches when she felt large hands at her waist.

Mark hauled her upright, and a crowd of anxious faces surrounded her immediately. "He's conscious and lucid," she reported. "One arm is broken. He doesn't have any other obvious injuries, but we need to get him to a trauma center as soon as possible. He could have closed-head or spinal injuries we can't see."

"A couple of you guys help me with this bush." Shel, the camp's handyman, came rushing around the side of the house with a power saw and his ever-present tool kit in his grip. He fired up the saw.

Over the roar of the motor, Mark yelled, "Wait!"

As Shel cut the power, Alice said, "We need towels."

"Here you go." Royce held up a stack of clean towels. "I figured you might need these."

"Good thinking," Alice said, smiling at the boy. She selected two of the largest and crawled beneath the bush again. "I'm going to cover you with these," she told Riley, "because we have to cut away the bush to get you out. It's going to sound hideous but I promise we won't hurt you."

"Okay. Man, Shel's gotta love this. He's been after Joe to let him cut down this stupid bush since one of the dogs got loose and hid out in here. No wonder it took us so long to catch it."

"It's a real jungle specimen," Alice agreed. She gently tucked the towels around Riley, making sure his head and face were well covered and yet allowed him plenty of space to breathe. "I'll be with you as soon as they move this bush, all right?"

"See you in five."

Once again, Alice crawled from beneath the shrubbery and once again, Mark assisted her to her feet. "Stand back here, Alice," he said, placing a hand at her back. "How's he doing?"

"Shocky, but doing okay, all things considered. We need to get him to a medical center though. That arm needs to be X-rayed."

Mark stepped forward with several other people as Shel revved up the saw and began to slice branches away. They had fetched safety glasses from somewhere and most of them wore gloves, a common sight throughout camp despite the heat. As Shel cut, his helpers held the branches so that nothing would fall on Riley. As quickly as he moved, they pulled away the brush.

Little by little, the shrub was denuded and Riley's shape could be seen beneath the towels. As soon as a space was opened, Alice knelt beside Riley again, disregarding the sawdust and the woodchips that bit into her knees. Quickly, she slipped a small board beneath the injured arm and bound it in the position it lay so that it could not be disturbed during transport.

Joe came along his other side. "Someone had a collapsible backboard so we're going to get you on it, buddy," he told Riley.

People surrounded them, and, on Joe's count, moved Riley carefully onto the backboard Joe had laid on the ground beside him, jostling him as little as possible. By now, Riley's face was so white that his spiky dyed hair looked neon yellow by contrast. Miranda brought Alice the first-aid kit, and she efficiently used bandages to immobilize his head against the board. She was relieved to see that there was no blood on the ground where he had lain.

One of the other volunteers backed a large SUV up to the site, and Royce, Mark and four other men lifted Riley into the back. Alice and Joe climbed in.

"Do you want the medical kit?" Miranda asked.

"No, you might need it here," Alice replied. She looked at all her new friends gathered around. "Nobody else can get hurt until I get back, okay?"

"You got it." Ellen closed the doors of the truck and they began to move.

"Are we going to a hospital?" Alice asked.

Joe shook his head. "The nearest one is almost an hour away. They've set up a trauma site just down the road, so we'll go there first."

"Just down the road" was nearly twenty minutes, Alice discovered. Thankfully, there was a doctor on site. Riley was examined and appeared to have sustained no injuries other than those found by Alice. An X-ray of the arm showed bones snapped cleanly in two.

During the X-ray exam, Alice noticed a young woman speaking on the public telephone nearby. Then the significance sank in. A public telephone!

"Look," she said to Joe. "I'm going to try to call home."

She walked to the phone as the young woman moved away. Thank heavens Jane had made her memorize her calling card information; she had rushed off without even taking her wallet. When she lifted the receiver, she rapidly punched in her sequences of numbers, following the prompts until at last she heard ringing.

"Grace Chapel Inn, Jane speaking. May I help you?"

"Hello, Jane. It's—"

"Alice! Hello! I'm so glad to hear from you. Not that I've been worried, but—"

"I'm sorry I couldn't call before. There hardly is any telephone service of any kind, mobile or landline, down here right now. Jane, you can't imagine the devastation: Signs are broken or missing; huge trees are just toppled right across the power lines and roads; entire roofs are torn away. We're at a camp twelve miles from the center of the hurricane zone, and I can't even imagine what it looks like closer in."

"So how are you managing a telephone call?"

"I came into town with another volunteer." Alice thought it might be better simply not to mention that she had brought in a patient who was injured at the camp. "The Red Cross has set up here, and power has been restored to a small area, so I thought I would call while I had a chance. How are all of you?"

"Fine, except that Louise and Aunt Ethel still aren't speaking," Jane reported. "Louise says Aunt Ethel should apologize for her unkind words, a position I agree with. Not that I expect it will ever happen. I haven't spoken about it to Aunt Ethel because . . . well, imagine the lecture I'd hear if I brought it up."

Alice sighed. "You'd get an earful, I guess."

"That's putting it mildly!"

"Is everything running smoothly at the inn?"

"Heavens, yes. We've had at least one room filled every night, and we are getting a lot more bookings for the holiday season than I expected. Oh, and I tried a new recipe that was a huge hit."

"Do tell."

"It didn't have any kind of catchy name, so I called it Grace Chapel Inn Egg Crunch. It was an easy one— hard-boiled eggs stuffed with a mixture of sour cream, crumbled bacon, halved olives, parsley and paprika. I served it with those vanilla-nutmeg muffins you like so well."

"Oh, stop. I'm consumed with envy. Down here we're making our meals on a camp stove."

Jane laughed. "So tell me more about Camp Compassion."

Where could she start to explain it all? Alice took a deep breath, knowing she never could convey adequately the experience she was having. "There are people here from all over the country. Some are from nearby, but the majority had to travel a long distance to get here. There are volunteers from Maine, Montana, Wisconsin, Texas…even California."

She went on, telling Jane every detail she could think of. Then she saw Joe go in the direction of the front desk. He came into view a moment later, hovering over Riley, who was walking slowly at his side. The injured arm was encased in a soft cast, which Alice knew would be exchanged for something more durable in a few days when the swelling had subsided. "I have to say good-bye now. My ride is ready to go."

"Oh, Alice, thank you so much for calling. Louise and everyone who has asked will be so glad to know you're doing all right. You're still planning to return Tuesday, right?"

"Right." Alice was silent for a moment. She could see that time was going to fly by. The thought of leaving saddened her. "Good-bye, Jane. Hug Louise for me. I love you."

Chapter Ten

By noon on Alice's fourth day in the disaster area, it was ninety-five degrees. It had not even cooled down much during the previous night, and everyone seemed to be moving a bit slower. The heat wave was unprecedented, and everyone was talking about how bad it could be for the animals caught in the hot, airless buildings.

Since Dr. Spade was nowhere in sight, Alice was assisting Gina in the CCU when Royce, one of Ellen's twins, came rushing through the door. "Alice, we just brought in a girl out here who collapsed. Joe needs you right now."

Alice glanced at Gina, who said, "Go, go!" She took the dog that Alice was about to return to a clean kennel. "I can handle this for a while. Thanks to you, we've already gotten through the morning rush."

Alice followed Royce into the supply room, where Joe was kneeling before a young woman lying on the couch. He wore a worried frown. "What does heat stroke look like?"

The people around the couch moved back to allow Alice space.

"Hello, I'm Alice." She sat on the edge of the couch and inspected her patient. "Can you tell me your name?"

The girl made an effort to smile. "Emilia. I'm from Boise. You know, Idaho."

"Idaho!" Alice was momentarily distracted. "That must have been a long drive."

The young woman rolled her eyes. "And then some. Luckily, there were three other people with me, so we all took shifts."

"Emilia, can you tell me what you are doing here?"

Emilia gave her a faintly puzzled stare. "Do you mean *here* as in 'at Camp Compassion,' here as in 'my specific duties' or here as in 'lying on this couch'?"

Alice smiled. It sounded as though the young woman was in full possession of her faculties. "Any of the above will do."

"I came to help with rescued animals. I help Corinne with the kennels, and I think I fainted."

Emilia's response was reassuring. Alice smiled at her patient. "How do you feel now that you're lying down?"

"A little sick to my stomach…and I have a really bad headache. It's been getting worse all day."

"Emilia, how much have you had to drink yesterday and today?"

The girl looked blank for a moment. "To drink? I don't know. A cup of water with breakfast is the only thing I can remember."

Alice looked up at Joe and the others anxiously hovering behind him. "I suspect this is heat exhaustion rather than heat stroke," she told him. "She's lucid, aware, pale and sweating heavily. Headache and nausea are common indicators. If this truly were a case of heat stroke, I would expect her to be a good bit more confused and she would be flushed rather than pale. Her breathing is fine too. Hyperventilating is a sign of heat stroke."

"Does she need to go to the hospital?"

"Let's try providing fluids, getting her on an IV and keeping her resting in this air-conditioned room. I'll keep an eye on her for any changes." Alice gestured to the stacks of supplies. "I saw a new arrival of medical items there, including some IV setups. Can someone find one for me?"

"I can tell someone where they are." The words came from Riley, who already was moving about the camp again, albeit carefully so as not to jar his injured arm.

In short order, what Alice had requested was handed to her. The only place she could find to hang the IV bag was from the chandelier over the table right in the middle of the room. The unorthodox setup made a statement, Alice thought, that defined the entire camp experience.

Alice had barely gotten Emilia settled when Joe and Kyle came through the door supporting a large man between them. Alice recognized Shel, the handyman.

"Hi, Alice," he said with a wave, although she could see Shel wasn't well.

"Lay him down over there." She pointed to a second couch against a wall.

"What were you doing today?" she asked Shel. He did not look as though he felt as bad as Emilia had.

"I was up on the roof again, patching some loose shingle. I started feeling woozy so I came down before I fell off."

"Smart decision, since we already have one patient who tried to do a bird imitation off that roof." She patted his shoulder as she teased him. "Some fluids should have you feeling better soon."

Joe hung around while she set up a second IV of saline solution and got Shel settled. Then she beckoned to Joe and stepped into the hallway, pulling the door closed behind her. "We need to keep that door closed so it stays cool in there. And we need to talk."

Alice was gentle and soft-spoken, but thanks to her nurse's training, she could infuse her voice with a no-nonsense note of command when necessary. "These people are not drinking enough. The only reason this hasn't happened earlier is because temperatures were cooler. But now it's unseasonably warm, and no one is taking that into account. They're all working like dogs."

Joe laughed. "Look around, Alice. The dogs here are definitely not the ones doing the work." But he sobered and pulled his clipboard in front of him. "So everyone needs to drink more."

"Yes."

"Any specific suggestions?" He looked up at her. "I do have some discretionary funds for things like water and ice."

"Good. Send someone into town for a cooler of ice and a couple cases of water bottles and maybe some of those energy drinks. Put them in a couple of big coolers in a central location and remind people to drink. Also, unless there's an urgent need, I'd recommend enforcing a mandatory break between noon and two, because some of these folks don't know the meaning of the word *rest*. In the meanwhile, let's spread the word about hydrating."

Mark came out of the CCU in time to catch the end of the conversation. "I told you she was fantastic," he said to Joe. Mark smiled at her, and she was flustered by the warmth in his eyes. "Thanks again for coming down here. It means a lot to me."

Joe hustled away with his clipboard, but Alice barely registered his withdrawal. "You're welcome," she said faintly. She supposed she always would care for Mark as more than simply a friend. For years, she had prayed for him to embrace his faith. Simply knowing that he was striving to be a better Christian each day made him doubly attractive to her. His presence brought her joy.

"So we're taking a break for a couple of hours in the afternoon?" he asked.

She nodded. "At least until it cools down. If we don't, I'm afraid there are going to be more people out of commission with heat-related problems."

Mark shook his head. "Aren't we a bunch? We put up awnings to shade the animals, refill water bowls and wading pools to keep them cool, then forget to take care of ourselves."

She laughed. "It sounds ridiculous when you put it that way."

"I have an idea," Mark said. "We could offer a Bible study during our downtime this afternoon."

"Oh yes." She was delighted that he'd thought of it. "June and I brought our Bibles, but I have to confess I was so exhausted the past few nights that I barely managed a short prayer before my eyes closed. A Bible study would be wonderful."

❦

Jane walked to the post office Friday morning. She donned a lightweight corduroy jacket over her scoop-necked

blue sweater and khaki pants. Her long dark hair was confined in a casual twist to prevent the wind from tangling it
unmercifully.

It was a beautiful, crisp fall day in Acorn Hill. A mild
breeze herded leaves in brilliant shades of red, yellow and
orange across the street in front of her. A wagon drawn by
a horse with a shining coat of ebony passed with a cluster of
laughing little girls snuggling into loads of loose, fragrant
hay. With its passing, the leaves swirled high into the air.

The scene reminded Jane of her childhood. It was a
pleasant reminiscence. She and her friends had raked huge
piles of leaves, ostensibly to help their neighbors. But mostly
the kids took turns leaping into the leaves, covering themselves completely, rolling around and giggling like mad.

$\backsim$

"Did you jump in the leaves when you were little?" she
asked Louise a few hours later as her eldest sister came into
the kitchen where Jane was working. Louise was dressed in
a long wool skirt and a twin set in a light blue similar to the
color of Jane's own sweater.

Louise stopped, one eyebrow rising as if to question
Jane's sanity. "Did I jump in the leaves?"

"Yes. You know, just for fun—rake up a big pile and
jump in them." She would not be surprised if Louise had

never enjoyed the delights of a fall leaf-leaping session. Her eldest sister seemed to have been born staid and responsible.

"Why on earth would I have wanted to do that?" Louise asked, her face perfectly expressionless.

"Didn't you—"

Louise burst out laughing. "Oh, Jane, I wasn't always stuffy, you know. Of course I jumped in the leaves when I was little. Didn't everybody?"

"You're not stuffy," Jane said loyally. "Just...serious, maybe."

"Serious. I like it."

"I'm glad you jumped in the leaves, Louie." The sisters gazed at each other for a moment, then burst into shared laughter.

When the merriment subsided, Louise asked, "What are you doing?"

Jane held up a lovely earring that glittered in shades of copper and bronze in the light. "Making some beaded jewelry for the crafts fair. I asked many other people to donate things, and it occurred to me that all I was planning to contribute were some baked goods."

"Jane, your baked goods are probably worth five of anything else we're selling."

"I doubt that, but thank you," Jane said, shaking her head modestly. "You know what I mean though."

"Have you gotten anything in yet, or are all the products still in the making?"

"Oh, wait until I show you!" Jane jumped up from her seat. "Things are starting to arrive." She headed for the stairs, speaking over her shoulder as Louise trailed behind her. "Of course, the group projects are not finished yet, and those are the bulk of the contributions, but some of the individual items are here. They're really lovely. Right now, I'm keeping it all in my bedroom. I'm a little concerned about where we are going to store everything. I thought I'd ask Aunt Ethel to talk to Kenneth about creating a screened-off corner in the Assembly Room, since we only need the space for about three weeks."

"That might work. Do you really expect to need that much space?" Louise followed Jane to the third floor, then stopped in the doorway of Jane's room.

All the pretty throw pillows that usually covered the little settee against one wall were lined up across the foot of Jane's bed. The seat itself was covered with boxes and piles of donated goods, and the open space beneath its slender legs also was filled to capacity.

"My dear heavenly days," Louise said. "I cannot believe you have gotten so much already. You definitely are going to have to find a larger area for everything." She walked across the room, drawn by the soft fabrics and colors of some of the needlework. "Look at this." She held up a shell-stitched afghan in shades of cream, palest lavenders and blues. "I don't have a place for this, but someone surely will have the perfect room. It's so beautiful!"

"Look at this." Jane held up a tiny pink hooded baby jacket and matching booties with big pom-poms attached. "Could it get any cuter?"

Louise refolded the afghan and turned to a delicate tablecloth of ecru thread shot with silver. "This is heirloom quality, Jane. If someone gave me something like this as a wedding gift, I would be thrilled. I am astounded that people have donated such costly items."

"Aunt Ethel's friends from the Seniors Social Circle are eager to do anything they can to make this a success. I think they were taken aback by the whole idea of putting a craft show together, but they have been going great guns making lovely things. And the best part is that all of these are strictly donations so any profit will go to the church, not to a vendor."

Jane and Louise admired the rest of the items, which included delicate tatted snowflake ornaments, a ruffled confection of a little girl's dress in soft pink that would be an instant hit with every grandmother who saw it, a quaint welcome plaque with a painstakingly detailed folk-art Santa, and plush, sweet-faced homemade teddy bears, among other things.

As they started down the steps, Jane said, "How is your Santa Lucia thingy coming along?"

"Very well, thank you. Yesterday I went over to the big library in Potterston to see what information I could gather on it, and you will never believe what I found."

"What?"

"A book in which several different ideas for these celebrations are included. But the best part is, there were several songs in the back for a wide variety of ages."

"What a stroke of luck!"

"Yes. I have to confess that after I let Kenneth talk me into this, I began to have some second thoughts about how I was going to put it all together in such a short time."

Jane grinned. "Seems as if everyone around here is worrying about getting things done on time."

"Perhaps not all of us," Louise remarked pointedly.

"Aunt Ethel excluded. Have you two talked yet?"

Louise shook her head, absently running her fingers over her pearls.

"You'll see her tomorrow. She's coming over to talk with me about the crafts fair."

Louise made a face. "Don't I have something to do tomorrow?"

"That's not nice," Jane informed her sister. "I'm about ready to make you two sit down in a very small room together until you make up."

Louise sighed. "I know I need to let go of it. I don't enjoy harboring anger or resentment toward anyone. But Jane, the things she said were really unkind."

"I know. But she's our only aunt, and who knows how long we'll have her with us? You would be sorry forever if you two weren't speaking and something happened to her."

Louise nodded. "But Jane," she pointed out, "it is rather difficult for me to speak to someone who is determined to pretend I do not exist."

❧

Temperatures still soared on Alice's fifth day with the animal-rescue group. As they had the day before, Alice, Mark and June held an informal Bible study beneath the shade of a canopy during the early afternoon break Joe had mandated. To Alice's delight, Ellen and the twins joined them, as did Gina and her friend Edmund, the third member of Mark's team.

The verse Alice chose to discuss came from 2 Corinthians: "So we fix our eyes not on what is seen, but on what is unseen. For what is seen is temporary but what is unseen is eternal" (4:18).

Alice posed a question for the group. She asked if the fact that life on earth is just a "temporary assignment" should change the way one is living and how. They just finished a lively discussion and a closing prayer when a group of people who had gone to town came walking past them.

"Did you pick up some ice?" Alice asked.

"Ice and water," Corinne replied. "I heard this heat is supposed to break on Sunday."

"Figures." Ellen slumped in her camp chair. "We're leaving Sunday."

"Hey, we're leaving Sunday too," another woman said, gesturing toward her companion. "We're taking dogs home, so we figure the return trip to Nevada is going to take close to three days if we stop at night. We want to be home for Thanksgiving."

"I have to be home for Thanksgiving too," Ellen murmured, as she raised her arms in a gesture of surrender. "I have fifteen people coming to my house for dinner!" Expressions of sympathy followed her announcement.

"We were planning to leave Monday," June said.

Several other camp volunteers made similar comments.

Finally, Mark chuckled. "Looks like I may be one of the few sticking around. Guess we'll be a little busier than usual."

"Sticking around for what?" Joe had come up behind Alice.

"Thanksgiving," Mark said.

"Oh. Yeah." Joe's voice was glum. "A lot of our volunteers are leaving to go home in time for Thanksgiving. It's going to be tough here. And frankly, I'm worried about how many volunteers we can count on after Thanksgiving and throughout the holiday season. It's all too easy for the world to forget disasters. Folks might assume our work is done."

"Why don't you ask every person leaving to try to send down a replacement?" Alice suggested. She knew that if she had not made the trip and seen firsthand the scope of the disaster's impact on pets, she might indeed assume help was no longer needed.

"That's a good idea!" Joe scribbled on his clipboard. "And I can ask them to post requests for help on some of the online bulletin boards too. If people understand that our need for assistance is going to last for many more weeks…"

"But that still doesn't solve your Thanksgiving problem," June pointed out.

"No, it doesn't." Joe's customary cheery facade slipped for a moment, and Alice saw the fatigue he hid so well much of the time. He straightened his shoulders. "Hanna, Corinne, Riley and I will be staying, as well as Mark, Gina, Edmund and a few of the volunteers. I guess we'll just have to manage somehow. No more intake, that's for sure."

"No more intake?" Alice was aghast. "But who will take the animals the teams find?"

"We won't send any teams in. Other shelters might, depending on how their volunteer rosters look."

Alice tried to hide her dismay as Joe went on his way. She suspected those shelters would be facing the same manpower crisis, which meant animals in need would not be rescued for days. She feared rescue might arrive too late for many of them. She had seen how thin and starving the latest arrivals had been. Further delay would cost the lives of who knew how many suffering pets. She could hardly bear to think of it. From their silence as others put their Bibles away and went back to work, she was pretty sure they felt the same way.

$\backsim$

The heat broke on Sunday, just as Corinne predicted.

When Alice awoke just before dawn and stepped out of her tent, the air was noticeably cooler and fresher. She should have been happy, but all she could think of was that she would be leaving in just one more day.

Ellen crawled out of her tent next door. "It's about time. Doesn't this cool air feel heavenly?"

"It does. Is there anything I can do to help you pack?" Alice recalled that Ellen and the twins were leaving today. "What time are you planning to leave?"

Ellen hesitated. Finally, she grinned and shrugged. "I don't think we're leaving. I drove into town last night and called my husband. There's so much need here that I wouldn't be able to enjoy a holiday meal. All I would be thinking about is how many dogs still need to be walked, how many animals need their meds, how many more still are out there waiting to be rescued. So I asked him to call my mother and sisters and see if they were all right with having dinner elsewhere—without us."

"And what did they say?"

"I don't know yet. We agreed that I'd drive into town again this morning after early chores and the morning meeting. I'll call him back to see if that plan would fly."

Alice was silent for a moment. "Would you mind if I rode along with you?"

Ellen's eyes lit with interest. "Any special reason?"

"I'd like to stay also," Alice confessed. "But it depends on how June feels, so I'll have to talk to her first."

"Talk to June about what?" Her friend stood yawning in the morning air. "Wow! It feels great out here. It'll be nice not to be a walking sponge all day."

Alice and Ellen both laughed.

Then Alice said, "Ellen has decided to stay longer if her family at home agrees." She hesitated. "How would you feel about staying longer?"

"You mean through the Thanksgiving holiday?"

Alice nodded hesitantly. "If possible."

"Oh, Alice, I'd love to!" June threw her arms around Alice in an exuberant hug. "It's all I've thought about since Joe talked to us yesterday. The folks at the Coffee Shop are okay with my staying longer. I was going to my son's in Philadelphia for the meal, but I know he and my daughter will understand when I explain." Her enthusiastic manner faded. "But what about your family?"

"My sisters will understand," she said. "My biggest question is going to be whether the hospital can manage without me a little longer."

"Well!" Ellen raised her coffee mug in a mock toast. "Let's hop on our chores, girls. Sounds like we have some telephone calls to make this morning!"

◡

Jane was tossing herbs together for the cranberry stuffing she intended to make later in the week when the telephone rang. Louise had gone to Karin Lindars' home to discuss plans for the Santa Lucia service, so Jane hurried to answer the call.

Grabbing a dishtowel to wipe her hands, she reached for the portable telephone on its cradle in the kitchen. "Grace Chapel Inn. This is Jane speaking. May I help you?"

"Jane?"

"Alice! Hello. How are you?"

"I'm fine."

But something in her sister's voice made Jane's mental antennae quiver. "No, you're not. What's wrong?" Her imagination began to run wild. "Were you hurt by an animal? Are you in a dangerous area? Is there—"

"Whoa!" Alice was laughing and Jane felt her tense muscles begin to relax. "I'm fine. Truly. Just a little nervous."

"Why are you nervous?"

"Is Louise home?"

The abrupt change of topic confused Jane. "Louise? Ah, no, she's meeting with Karin again. Why?"

"I have something to ask you both. But this may be my only chance to get to a telephone for several more days, so I suppose I'll have to run it by you and let you explain to Louise."

"All right. Shoot." Jane could not imagine what Alice could —"Oh no. No, no, no. You can't bring animals home, Alice. Absolutely not. You know what Louise will say. Not to mention poor Wendell. He is king of the castle around here, and I cannot imagine he would be happy to have to share with another animal."

"That's not it." Alice chuckled again. "At least, not right now. Goodness, you have a vivid imagination." Her voice sobered. "It's about Thanksgiving. Jane, would you be terribly upset if June and I stayed down here an extra week?"

"An extra week? That's…that's a long time. Can you take that much time away from work?"

"I already checked and they said they can manage. I guess I'm lucky that my supervisor is an animal lover. She told me it was no trouble. June has no problem with staying, but if you're swamped at the inn, I'll come home."

There was a short silence. "You're needed there so much?"

"Very much. A great many of the volunteers are leaving to get home in time for Thanksgiving, and they are going to be understaffed here through next weekend."

"I'm sure they will be," murmured Jane. Then she paused. "What's that Karen Carpenter song we used to like? '(There's No Place Like) Home for the Holidays.'"

"There isn't. But I've prayed about this, and I feel that it is what God wants from me. I know it's a lot to ask, and I will miss sharing the meal with you terribly, but I believe this is one of the most important missions I have ever participated in, Jane. I wish you could be here to see the change in the animals as they begin to recover from their ordeal."

Jane thought about it. "Oh, Alice, you have to follow your heart. If you feel called to stay, then who am I to tell you not to listen? God will accept your thanks and praise just as easily in Florida as He will if you're sitting at home with your family. Louise and I will miss you, but it sounds as if you're needed down there."

"Oh, Jane, thank you. Do you think Louise will understand?"

"I do. She's going to be disappointed, but I know she'll support you, Alice."

"Thank you, Jane. Thank you so much. I'll try to call again before Thanksgiving, but if you don't hear from me, don't worry. June and I plan to leave for home a week from tomorrow."

Chapter Eleven

Upon their return to camp, Alice, June and Ellen were barely out of the car when Ellen's children came charging toward them.

"What did Dad say, Mom?"

"Can we stay?"

Ellen kept her eyes downcast as she unbuckled her seatbelt and opened the door. Alice watched, puzzled.

"Oh man," Royce said. "He said we have to come home, didn't he?"

"No! We can't leave," Miranda protested. "Joe and the others need us. There are too many animals for them to take care of. Oh, Mom, you have to go back to town. Take me and let me talk to him." Miranda's voice was impassioned and Alice could feel her distress.

Ellen stood. "He said…we can stay!" She threw open her arms on the last words and laughed as both teens ran to her, hugging her wildly even as they scolded her for teasing them.

Behind the children, Alice saw Mark approaching. His blue eyes were questioning as he looked at her. "What did your sisters say?"

"Louise wasn't home, so I only spoke to Jane. But she was wonderfully understanding when I explained that I've been praying about it and I feel compelled to stay. June's children also said they didn't mind if she stayed, so I guess the five of us will be with you through Thanksgiving."

Mark's smile warmed her clear down to her toes. "Fantastic!"

"I'm going to tell Joe," Miranda announced. "He's going to be so happy."

Alice walked quickly back to the CCU. Although she had not had any heat-exhaustion patients in the past day or so, she liked to be aware of any medical issues that cropped up. Besides, Gina might need her help.

The object of her thoughts was seated on the steps of the house as Alice approached.

"Hey, Alice," Gina called. "How did you guys make out?"

"Ellen, the kids, June and I all are staying through the Thanksgiving weekend," Alice reported.

"That's terrific!" Gina also was going to be staying, for which Alice was thankful. She could not imagine how upset Dr. Spade would be if he learned that his one technician was going to leave and he would have no other help but

Alice. "Hey," Gina was saying, "would you see if you can get that shepherd in the bottom left-hand corner to eat?"

"He still hasn't eaten?" Alice was aghast.

Gina shook her head glumly. "I've tried everything. Even Dr. Spade has tried, but he just turns his head away."

"Poor baby," Alice said. She was worried. The shepherd couldn't afford to miss a single meal. His hold on life was tenuous at best, and if he didn't eat soon, he might not recover. "Could they put in a feeding tube?" That was usually the next step with human patients who were not eating.

"We don't have the medical staff or the resources to monitor an animal with a feeding tube. Besides, he's already in such bad condition that surgery probably would kill him."

"I'll sit with him," Alice offered. "I don't know if I can do anything for him, but I can try."

She went inside and washed her hands. After making certain there were no human medical problems, she moved on to the CCU. To her relief, Dr. Spade was not about. Mark soon joined her and briefed her on the shepherd's condition.

"I can't find anything drastically wrong," he said. "We don't have the resources here for exploratory surgery. But my instinct tells me he doesn't need surgery. I think he's dying of a broken heart."

"A broken heart. Can that really happen?" But she knew it could. She had seen it in human patients throughout her years of nursing. People just gave up. It only made sense that the same thing could happen with an animal.

"It's a disease of the spirit," Mark said. "As a veterinarian, I hate to say there's nothing I can do, but I'm at a loss. All we can do is pray." He put a hand on her shoulder and squeezed gently. "Don't feel too bad if you don't succeed. We can't save them all."

But Alice was determined to try. Mark left to examine another animal while she prepared a bowl of soft food and carried it to the kennel.

As she approached the sick dog, she was filled with sympathy. The shepherd lay listlessly. It did not even lift its head, although its eyes flicked briefly in her direction. Alice opened the kennel door and sat down on the recently cleaned floor just outside the kennel.

"Hey, buddy," she whispered. "How would you like something to eat?" She reached in a fisted hand and held it before the dog's nose, letting the animal get her scent, but the dog still did not stir. "What's the matter?" she asked. "Are you missing your folks? I bet somebody loves you very much."

She could not comprehend an owner who would go away and leave this beautiful animal behind, but in all fairness, she recognized that many coastal residents were so used to hurricanes that did not become dangerous in their area that they often were lackadaisical about evacuation. This dog's family probably expected to be home again by dinnertime. The card on the front of the cage gave an address and the circumstances under which the animal had been found. This was the dog, she recalled, that had been found lying in the wreckage of a collapsed home.

"Come on, boy," Alice said. She waved the food before the dog, but there was no response. After several futile attempts, she reached into the bowl and got some food on her fingers. She was aware that she did not know this dog, but she felt no menace. *Lord*, she prayed, *help me. Use my hands to save this life*. But after thirty minutes, she saw no evidence that the shepherd was interested in eating, even from her open hand.

Then an idea occurred to her. Maybe the dog would eat if he didn't have to expend any effort in the process. Leaving the kennel, Alice prepared a liquid gruel of high-calorie dog food and filled a large syringe with it. The syringe had a blunt tip for feeding rather than a needle at its end.

She returned to the kennel, this time reaching in to move the shepherd. She lifted the massive head into her lap and began to stroke the dog's soft fur, tracing the lovely markings and fondling the large, upright ears that were wilted back against its skull. "Let's try a little food, buddy," she coaxed. Taking the syringe, she held it to the corner of the dog's mouth and carefully depressed the plunger just far enough to squeeze a small amount of food along the dog's gum line.

Still, the dog didn't respond. Even though there was food lying right in his mouth, he wouldn't make the effort.

Alice's heart sank. "Come on, boy," she said. "You can't quit. What if your family's coming back? I bet they're searching everywhere for you. You can't let them down. You made it this far." She bent her head and brushed a kiss across the crown of the dog's head.

And she felt the shepherd move. Afraid to make a sudden gesture that might startle the dog, she strained to see out of the corner of her eye. What she saw made her heart swell with gratitude. The dog had licked his chops and the food Alice gave him was gone.

Thank You, Lord. Thank You so much.

Lifting her head, Alice squeezed another small bit of food out, and this time, the dog licked its mouth right away. On the third try, he actually stirred, lifting his head for a second before laying it back in Alice's lap.

The door of the CCU opened. Mark and Dr. Spade came in, discussing how best to treat a wound. She heard Mark's soft exclamation and then both sets of footsteps stopped, but she was afraid to move too much.

"Alice?"

"Hi. He's eating," she whispered.

"That woman shouldn't be reaching in there." Dr. Spade kept his voice low, but there was anger in his tone. "All we need is for one of these people to get bitten and sue the pants off of every rescue organization imaginable."

"Alice wouldn't do that," Mark said. "Besides, I don't believe she's going to get bitten. Look."

The shepherd's tail had begun a slow wave back and forth across the blanket as Alice fondled the thick ruff at its neck. She held the syringe against the side of the dog's mouth and depressed the plunger again, and this time, the white teeth parted, allowing Alice to squirt some food directly into its mouth.

"Let's let them alone." Mark's voice was low and gentle.

"All right," Dr. Spade responded. Then he looked down at Alice. "Please be careful. We can't afford to lose our hardest worker."

Both men turned and quietly left the critical care unit while Alice sat there staring. Had Dr. Spade just said something kind? Something complimentary? She raised her hand and pretended to check her own fore-head for fever. "You must have imagined that," she said to herself.

She bent over and kissed the shepherd again. "What a good boy you are. Let's finish this up, and maybe you can eat some out of a bowl."

Reaching for the bowl she'd prepared earlier, she set it in the kennel and was thrilled to see the dog lift his head and sniff the food. He wasn't standing, but that didn't surprise her, given his weak and emaciated appearance. "Eat up, buddy," she murmured.

Just then, a single sharp yip sounded behind her. Alice turned around. Her little friend from her first night of intake, the black-and-white cocker spaniel, was on her feet, nose pushed as far as possible through the openings of her kennel. Her entire posture shouted, "Hey! What about me?"

"Did you think I forgot you? You're still my favorite girl." Alice walked over and knelt before the kennel. "I'm going to feed you and take you out for a walk in a little while."

The little dog stood on its hind legs against the bars. In that position, Alice could see the ugly tumor that marred its soft underbelly. She prayed every evening that the tumor was benign and that the cocker would have plenty of years left. But Mark had not been any more optimistic than Dr. Spade had in his assessment of the tumor, and Alice feared the worst.

Louise held the first rehearsal for the Santa Lucia celebration the Tuesday evening before Thanksgiving. Rev. Thompson had announced it from the pulpit for the previous two Sundays, and Louise also had placed the notice in the bulletin about it last week.

She looked on anxiously as the chapel began to fill with children at seven, the designated time for the group to gather. If no one came, the Lindars family might not feel very welcome at Grace Chapel. Louise thought the Santa Lucia celebration would be a lovely addition to the church's Advent preparations and hoped others would feel the same way.

Not long after seven, Louise began to see that her fears were groundless. First to arrive were the Lindars: Karin and her three youngest children, Marit, Niklas and Mattias. They had not even removed their coats when Charles and Sissy Matthews, two of Louise's piano students, arrived. A steady procession of children followed: Many of Alice's ANGELs came, including Kate Waller, who brought her seven-year-old sister Abby; and Sarah Roberts, looking totally disgusted as her younger brother Eason came in making lots of noise. Louise put a quick stop to Eason's outbursts.

Briana and Tiffany Sherman arrived next, followed immediately by the two youngest Dawson boys and another brother and sister from the congregation. Louise and Karin both winced as the rowdy Trimble brothers, both in fourth grade, burst through the door.

As she surveyed the group of participants, Louise took a deep breath. That block of eight- and nine-year-old boys bore close watching, but she was delighted that nearly two dozen of the chapel's children had turned out for this. There was a paucity of older boys, whose mothers probably hadn't been able to bribe, threaten or force them to attend, so the older group consisted of the ANGELs and a few other girls.

As the children took seats in the pews, Louise offered a simple explanation of Saint Lucy's good works, Swedish customs that Karin had told her about and the theme of light they would use in their service.

"All right, then, boys and girls. We'll start with the song we all will sing together. Almost all of the songs we will learn are titled 'Santa Lucia,' so I shall refer to this one by its first line: 'Hark! Through the darksome night.'"

"*Darksome*'s not a word," chortled one of the Trimble boys.

"It most certainly is, young man." Louise's voice brooked no argument. "These songs were written many years ago when people often spoke and wrote differently than we do today."

The Trimble child became silent, and Louise sat down at the piano to begin the introduction as the vocal rehearsal went on. After twenty minutes, Louise felt satisfied with their progress. The children had made a good start on "Hark! Through the Darksome Night," and "Santa Lucia, Thy Light Is Glowing," a simpler tune that could be sung in a round. She had made copies of the songs for each child to take home, and she intended to pass these out at the end of the rehearsal.

After a short break, Karin lined up the children in order of height. Louise had worried a bit about how to deal with the fact that this whole ceremony was created so that Marit Lindars could be a Lucia. Fortunately, Marit was the tallest of the gaggle of young girls, so it made perfect sense that she would wear the crown this year. And since no one had seen a Santa Lucia program before, the other girls all seemed thrilled to be handmaidens.

Louise figured that if this became an annual tradition, she would hereafter let Rev. Thompson deal with what was sure to become a thorny issue of choosing a Lucia.

⁓

Camp Compassion was quiet without the customary complement of volunteers. Wednesday evening, Alice, June, Ellen and the twins were sitting around a small campfire they had made when the evening's work was done. Providing care had been difficult with so few people, and everyone handled at least half a dozen animals.

Coming at the end of the day's toil, the final hours were exhausting.

"I have to make one more trip over to the CCU," Alice said, "and then I'm turning in. The next couple of days are going to be challenging."

"You can say that again." Miranda flopped down in a camp chair and fanned herself dramatically. "We're going to be working twice as hard as we did before."

"Based on the premise that there are only half as many of us left?" Her brother grabbed the back of the chair and pretended to tip her over.

"Royce!" Miranda's arms and legs flailed. Fortunately, her twin was only teasing, and he steadied the chair with both hands, returning all four legs to the ground as she clutched at his arms.

"Those two." Ellen shook her head fondly. "Sometimes I'm not sure if they're seventeen or seven," she said to Alice.

The camping area was oddly quiet. Alice had been used to hearing the murmur of low conversations, the metallic sounds of cooking over camp stoves and even the snores of their louder neighbors.

Now, the two little tents looked like an oasis in the middle of a desert. There were a few other tents still dotting the field, and the RV was still there. Mark's mobile clinic was parked near the house, and Alice knew he had been sleeping there, as had Edmund, while Gina bunked with one of the other women.

"I may have to break down and take a shower in the morning," June said. "Do you think we can manage to rig that shower up long enough to take turns?"

"We can hold the darn thing up if we have to," Ellen said. "I think a shower is an excellent idea." The shower enclosure had proven impossible to keep in place, and after two campers suffered embarrassment at the mercy of the unpredictable frame, attempts at showers were abandoned. But now that there were so few people about, cleaning up seemed less risky.

"I think we could do it if two of us hold the curtain in place while the third showers."

"Oh, that would be heavenly." June hugged herself. "My daughter didn't believe me when I said I hadn't had a shower in a week."

"Sponge baths and baby wipes can only help so much," Ellen muttered.

Alice laughed. "I've got snarls in my hair that may never come out."

"Peanut butter works," offered Miranda.

All three women turned and looked at her.

"Peanut butter?" echoed her mother.

"Yeah. You work it into the knotted part and just gently start teasing pieces lose. It worked wonders when I got a barrette caught in my hair in eighth grade."

"Why didn't I know about this?" Ellen said to the sky.

"Because Faith and I were fooling around, and I was afraid you'd get mad. It worked, so no problem, right?"

"I think I'll pass on the peanut-butter solution." Alice indicated her practical, chin-length hairstyle. "This doesn't require anything quite that drastic."

She rose from her chair and slipped off the rubber sandals she had been wearing around the tent area. Jamming her feet into her still-tied sneakers, she said, "I'll be back in a little while. I want to see if I can get that poor shepherd to eat a little more."

"I'll walk you over," Royce offered. "It's easy to trip over that rough ground in the dark." He rose, picking up a wide-beamed flashlight.

"Thank you." Alice was grateful for the young man's thoughtful concern. Walking through a bumpy field at night was challenging, and she appreciated the company.

Without further delay, she and Royce headed for the house. After he saw her to the door, he walked down the lane to visit with Kyle, the security man, for a few moments.

Alice stepped into the dim light of the CCU after she mixed up a bowl of the soft food she wanted to give the shepherd. All the dogs were quiet. The ones who had been there for a while were either too sick to notice her or too content in their safe environment to bark, and three new patients still were disoriented and subdued from their ordeal. Very few were in the same condition that they had been in when she arrived more than a week earlier. Rescue groups and departing volunteers made a daily dent in the number of animals at the camp, but each evening at intake, those numbers swelled again.

"Hey, my big boy." Alice gently stroked the dog's head as she set down the bowl. This evening, the shepherd lifted his head and looked alert, his ears up, providing an inquisitive appearance. "I brought you a snack to hold you through the night. Eat up." Mark had warned her not to feed the dog large amounts at a time because its stomach had been empty for so long. Since her midafternoon victory, Alice had fed the dog two more small amounts of food.

The shepherd immediately started licking at the bowl of food. Alice backed away, happy to see the dog eating so well on his own.

A whining sound behind her made her smile. "You can't stand it when I pay attention to someone else, can you?" she asked the cocker spaniel. Its pink tongue hung out. The small black-and-white dog had been there the longest, Alice was sure. Several times, Alice had seen rescue groups ready to take her until they saw the tumor. One woman even intended to take her despite it—until the little dog growled at the lady.

Alice opened the kennel door and sat down on the floor, and the cocker jumped into her lap as if she'd been doing it for years. "You're someone's pet. Somebody loved you." She stroked the dog's ears and scratched her neck, chuckling when the dog immediately rolled onto her back. Alice rubbed the smooth belly, keeping her hands well away from the tumor.

A quiet voice behind her nearly made her jump. "She loves that, doesn't she?"

Mark. Alice relaxed as he lowered himself to the floor beside her, propping his back against the wall. "She seems to. I keep thinking someone must have loved her. She's obviously used to being cuddled." She indicated the dog now settling down on her lap.

"Sure seems like it." Mark reached over to fondle the cocker's ears but quickly withdrew his hand when the little dog curled her lip and uttered a warning growl.

"Stop that! He's your friend. And mine."

"Yours, certainly, but I'm not sure how many of the rest of us she likes," he said, and she heard a hint of laughter in his tone. "What's she going to do when you leave?"

Alice had already begun to worry about that very thing. "I don't know. I keep hoping her owners will come for her." Several times during the week, people seeking their pets had walked through the camp. On two occasions, there had been joyous reunions. But far more often, tears had flowed as hopes were dashed yet again. "Mark?"

"Yes?" He was watching the German shepherd still licking at its food.

"Will this tumor metastasize?"

He frowned. "There is no way to know without a biopsy. But I have to tell you, Alice, it has the classic look of a slow-growing malignancy." He glanced down at the dog, lying contentedly on her back in Alice's lap. "Look at her. She was somebody's baby. An indoor pet, from the look of her coat."

"How could they have let that tumor go?" Outrage quivered in her voice. She couldn't stand the thought of a helpless animal suffering. It had no way to explain its pain. It depended on people to care for it and to love it.

"Perhaps her owners had no choice. Parts of this area are very economically depressed. People with no money can love their pets just as dearly as the local millionaire but be unable to afford veterinary care." He indicated the kennels. "You saw how many of them haven't been spayed or neutered. And I suspect that when they're examined, a number of them will have Lyme disease or be heartworm positive."

"Goodness. Thanks, Dr. Graves, for that positive assessment."

He smiled, tipping his head back to rest it against the wall. "Sorry. I know you too well to sugarcoat anything. You'd realize I was lying in a heartbeat."

Alice was silent. The moment felt oddly intimate, sitting together in the dim light of the small room, speaking in hushed tones. Could her life have been full of this kind of sharing if she had married Mark? She might have a grandchild in her lap instead of a rescued animal.

"Alice?"

"Yes?"

"Do you ever wish . . . that you'd done things differently?"

She smiled. "I was just thinking about that. You do know me well." She took a deep breath, understanding what he was asking. Did she regret not deepening their relationship all those years ago? "Sometimes I wonder about it. My life has been satisfying. Happy, for the most part. I know people wonder how I could have been content as a spinster living with my elderly father. But they weren't on the inside. Our lives were busy and fulfilling. Father, with my help, made a positive difference in so many lives for many years. Do I wish I'd done things differently? No, I don't believe so. But I wouldn't be human if I didn't wonder what the path not taken might have led to."

"I wonder sometimes too." His voice was low. "But now I believe our lives have been just as they were meant to be.

Each of us has a purpose, as we discussed the other day in our Bible study."

There was a comfortable silence between them.

"You know I've spoken of retiring, of perhaps working part-time in a small companion-animal practice."

"From treating elephants to being a small-town vet. Quite a change."

He chuckled quietly. After a pause, he said, "I suppose what I would like to know is if you...have you ever considered whether I might be a part of your future?"

They were silent again. Alice continued to stroke the cocker spaniel. Finally, she said, "You have always held a special place in my heart. You know that. Right now I feel committed to making Grace Chapel Inn a success with Louise and Jane." She took a deep breath. "If you ever retire—which I will believe when I see a letter to that effect—I would be interested in spending more time with you."

Mark did not say anything.

"I wish I could give you a more definitive answer," she said, unable to read his silence. "But I can't decide in advance how I might feel about something that may or may not ever happen."

"I understand. Perhaps there will be time for another conversation like this in our future." He reached over and lightly covered her free hand with his. The cocker spaniel growled, and he chuckled as he released Alice. "I feel as if I have a chaperone." He got to his feet and stood looking down at her for a long moment.

"Mark?"

"Yes?"

"Whatever the future holds, I hope you know how much I treasure your friendship."

"And I yours. Good night, Alice."

"Good night, Mark."

She put away the cocker spaniel and removed the empty food bowl from the shepherd's kennel, praising the dog for eating. She was greatly encouraged by that.

Royce was just returning when she stepped outside. Gratefully, she accepted his company on the walk back to their campsite, all the while mentally replaying Mark's words.

Her prayers that night included wellness for the shepherd as well as for guidance in her relationship with Mark Graves.

Chapter Twelve

Thanksgiving Day began much like any other at Camp Compassion except that there were fewer hands to tackle the work. The group had decided to have a meal together midafternoon, after the lunch chores and before all the animals required evening feeding and attention.

Alice was cleaning kennels midmorning when she heard shouting and commotion outside. Instinct had her rising to her feet and rushing to the door. As she did, two people came toward her supporting a third between them. The person appeared to be cradling one hand with the other, and his shirt was smeared with blood.

"What happened?" She already was pulling on rubber gloves from one of the boxes Joe had insisted be kept all over the camp.

"Dog bite."

Dear heaven. It was one of the things they all feared most.

One of the volunteers said, "Those doggone pit bulls—"

"Had nothing to do with this." Corinne sent the speaker a glare. "It was a Labrador retriever."

"Sit him down here, and someone stay close in case he passes out."

"Blood doesn't bother me," the young man said. He grimaced. "But bite marks do." Alice had to search her memory for a moment, but finally his name came to her.

"Foster, right? You've been working with Corinne on the bigger dogs."

He nodded.

Alice knelt in front of him. "All right, let me take a look at that hand, Foster."

The young man took a deep breath and extended his hand.

The dog had gotten a real hold on him, leaving open wounds on both the front and the back of his hand. At her request he wiggled his fingers and thumb, holding back a cry of pain as he did so.

"Excellent," Alice said. "Your fingers are okay, and it looks like everything works." Gently she used a gauze pad to wipe the blood away. The wounds were not as deep as they could have been, and she did not think the dog's teeth had nicked any vital blood vessels. Still, the bleeding needed to be halted.

She stacked several gauze pads together and laid them over the wounds. "I'm going to put pressure on this for a minute," she warned him.

He nodded. "Okay."

Kyle was one of the people who had brought him in, and the beefy security guard extended a hand to Foster. "Here," he said. "Squeeze if you need to."

"Thanks, man." Foster bit his lip and screwed up his face as Alice began to press on the wound.

"You're going to need to see a doctor," she said. "And quarantine that dog," she added to those behind her.

"Already taken care of," Joe said.

Foster shuffled his feet.

Carefully, Alice lifted the gauze away from his wound and was gratified to see the bleeding had slowed to a sluggish trickle. She cleaned the area with antiseptic and wrapped the hand in clean bandaging. "Off to the hospital we go."

As before, Alice and her patient piled into a truck with Joe and zipped off to the medical clinic. Alice kept an eye on Foster, tucking a blanket around him to keep him warm as a precaution against shock.

Alice made a beeline for the telephone once Foster had been admitted into the ER and whisked away. She punched the buttons with a trembling finger, eager for the sound of home.

"Grace Chapel Inn, Louise speaking. May I help you?"

"Only if you're prepared to drive to Florida."

"Alice!" Louise put aside her usual composure; she sounded like a giddy girl. "Oh, it's so wonderful to hear your voice. We miss you so much."

"I miss you too." Alice had to clear her throat. "Happy Thanksgiving. I wish I wasn't missing Jane's pumpkin pie and all the other goodies I know you're having."

"And we wish you were here with us. But I agreed with Jane when she told you to stay. We know you must really be needed to even consider missing Thanksgiving."

"I do. There's still a steady stream of animals being brought out."

"Tell me about your experiences. I got a secondhand story from Jane before."

"Where is Jane?"

"Oh! She's in the kitchen. Let me go tell her to pick up the extension so she can listen too."

It was wonderful to hear Jane's voice again. Alice missed her sisters terribly. She told them about her little cocker friend with the tumor, about her victory earlier with the shepherd, and about the pregnant rottweiler. She tried to convey how close she felt to Ellen, to Royce and Miranda and Corinne, to Gina, Joe and Mark, and even to

Dr. Spade, to everyone else with whom she was working. She was aware that her words weren't able to paint a true picture, but she did her best. The one thing she did not mention was Foster's dog bite. That probably was not a detail that would inspire Jane and Louise to believe her declaration that she was safe.

All too soon, she had to end the conversation. "But I'll be home in five days," she assured them. "And this time I mean it."

"You'd better be," said Jane. "I need some reinforcements to help me deal with Aunt Ethel."

"Gee," said Alice. "I believe I hear an ulterior motive hidden in there."

Louise laughed. "Oh, it's not hidden. Alice, she is driving Jane mad. I actually feel lucky that she isn't speaking to me."

"Still?" Alice was shocked.

"Still." Louise sounded more resigned now than upset. "Please come home. You're much better at keeping her calm and focused than either of us."

The conversation ended on a happy note a few moments later, and Alice turned to find Joe standing at the door of the waiting room waving the car keys at her. They didn't linger at the hospital as they had before, because a doctor informed them that they were going to keep Foster overnight. Apparently, there was some question about possible nerve damage, and they wanted to evaluate him further.

❧

Back at camp after returning from the hospital, Alice found that Corinne had cleaned up the bloody, gauze-littered area Alice left behind when they took Foster to the hospital.

After providing a brief account of Foster's treatment, Alice asked, "How, exactly, did it happen?"

"A freak accident," Corinne said. "Foster went into the Lab's run to give him a bowl of food. He tripped over a blanket and nearly fell, but caught himself. Unfortunately, he dropped the food bowl, and when he bent to pick it up, I guess the Lab thought he was taking it away, and wham! The dog nailed him."

Alice winced. "Oh, what a shame for both of them."

"Yes, because that seemed to be a nice dog otherwise. Now we're going to have to record that he has a bite history and can be food aggressive, which reduces his chances of adoption significantly. And let's face it, I wouldn't want to be responsible for adopting him out to a family and learning that he'd hurt a child, would you?"

Alice shook her head. "That would be terrible. I wonder if the dog really is food aggressive or was just frightened."

"We'll never know. But he just came in last night, so he has good reason to be pretty freaked out. If you'd been starved for three weeks and someone gave you food, then started to take it away, what would you do?"

"I'd probably fight for the food."

"Exactly. I'm pretty sure that's what happened. The dog perceived a threat to his food source. I'm going to be watching him carefully for evidence of food aggression as he gets used to being fed regularly and doesn't feel hungry."

Corinne headed for the door. "Back to work for me. I want to tell the rest of the kennel workers how Foster is doing. They're anxious."

"That's very understandable."

"Hey, Alice." Gina beckoned to her from the doorway of the critical care room. "I have something to show you."

Something in Gina's manner made Alice smile. Whatever it was, it was good news of some sort. She hurried into the CCU. "What is it?"

"Look." Gina pulled her to the kennel at the end, the kennel over which they had draped towels yesterday.

Alice lifted one of the towels and peered in. The rottweiler lay on her side. Nestled against her was a mass of tiny, wriggling puppies.

"She had them!" Alice was delighted. She knelt and counted. "Seven?"

Gina nodded. "They don't look preterm, and they're all pretty lively. She cleaned them up right away and has started feeding them."

"They're precious." Something positive like this was what she had needed after the unfortunate bite accident. Alice dropped the towel back into place and stood. "I can see it's going to be hard to get anything done. I'm going to be tiptoeing over there for a peek every five minutes."

Gina laughed. "I know. She—Alice! Look!"

Alice turned to see why Gina was so excited.

There, standing in its kennel, albeit on wobbly legs, was the German shepherd Alice had fed the night before. Its tail was waving tentatively back and forth.

"Oh, baby boy." Alice went over, opened the door of the kennel door and knelt. The dog took a tentative step forward and pressed his broad head against Alice's chest. "What a good boy you are. You're doing so well." She cuddled the big dog for a little while, marveling. True, she loved animals, but if anyone had told her she would be sitting in front of a German shepherd with a mouthful of teeth inches from her face, she would have refused to believe it.

Gina came up beside her with a bowl of the soft food they had mixed for the big dog. "Work your magic, O Great One," she said with a grin.

Alice chuckled. "As if you haven't worked a few miracles of your own in here." She put the bowl before the shepherd but was disappointed when the dog turned its head away. "I know you like this stuff," she said to the big dog. "You ate it last night."

She maneuvered the bowl around in front of the dog several times, but no luck. Finally, Alice said, "If only you knew how much I hate this," and she scooped her hand into the bowl of food. She held her palm beneath the shepherd's nose. "See? You've got your very own serving woman. Now come on, buddy, let's eat." She was rewarded when the dog gently took the food from her hand.

Behind her, Alice heard a quiet yet victorious "Yes!" and she was sure Gina had just pumped her fist into the air as she was wont to do.

Someone else entered the room. "How did she get that dog to eat?" Alice heard Dr. Spade's voice.

"Isn't it amazing?" Gina was cheery and enthusiastic. "Lots of TLC."

Dr. Spade went over to check on the rottweiler and her pups. "Looks like everybody's doing fine in there." It was the first time Alice had heard anything approaching satisfaction in his voice and she smiled as she continued feeding the shepherd. "I actually came in here for a reason," the vet said. "I'm supposed to tell you the meal is almost ready. Round up your troops for Thanksgiving dinner."

He turned and walked out, and Alice swiveled until her gaze met Gina's.

"Wow!" said Gina. "He was almost normal."

Thanksgiving at Grace Chapel Inn was odd without Alice, Louise decided. That was the only word for it. *Odd*.

Jane had invited their aunt and her special friend Lloyd Tynan for the meal even though Louise and Ethel were still at odds. Jane had mentioned the meal to Sylvia Songer, whom she feared might be alone on Thanksgiving Day, and Louise had learned that Kenneth Thompson also would be on his own, so she invited him. They had two guests from the inn, an older gentleman as well as a young woman who taught in a private school, whom the two sisters had agreed to invite to share in their feast. Then Jane, in a burst of magnanimity that Louise suspected she was beginning to regret a bit, had called Florence and Ronald Simpson. Having no children of their own, she suspected they did not have plans. When Florence accepted with alacrity, she realized her suspicions had been correct.

They decided to serve relatively traditional fare. Jane had stuffed and baked a turkey and was now whipping buttermilk potatoes into a frothy delight. Her special cranberry-orange sauce was ready to go on the table, as were several vegetables and homemade honey-wheat biscuits. She had made both pumpkin and lemon-meringue pies, as well as a selection of cookies for those too full for an entire slice of pie. Louise felt a bit guilty for not helping with more of the preparation, but Jane assured her she didn't need to. And, thought Louise, watching her little sister efficiently buzzing from one dish to another, Jane was so very good at it.

Louise had set the table with their mother's best china, a soft, lovely Wedgwood pattern, and was filling a crystal pitcher with water when the doorbell rang.

"Our first guests." She set the pitcher aside. "I'll get that."

Florence and Ronald Simpson were the first arrivals. As she took their coats, Louise could see Ethel Buckley and Lloyd Tynan just pulling into the driveway. She hurried back to the kitchen.

"You've got to come in here," she said to Jane. "Aunt Ethel and Florence in the same room? Are we prepared for that? And I certainly can't help since Ethel isn't speaking to me."

"I talked with Aunt Ethel," Jane assured her. "She promised to try to make Florence feel that her contributions to the crafts fair are important."

"I wish Kenneth would get here," Louise said fervently as the doorbell rang the second time. "He handles those two better than anyone else I know, even Alice."

The sisters were silent for a moment, thinking of their absent one. Alice was the acknowledged peacekeeper in the family and beyond, with her soft demeanor and kind words.

Louise sometimes wished she could be more like Alice. But honestly, there was simply no reason for some of the silly things people did, and she had limited patience. Alice had been born to soothe, which was one reason she was such an excellent nurse.

"Happy Thanksgiving!" Louise exclaimed.

"And the same to you," Lloyd returned. "Thank you for inviting me.

Ethel only mumbled a holiday greeting, and Louise's smile faded. Avoiding her aunt's eyes, she beckoned the couple into the foyer. "Let me take your coats. Kenneth, do come in," she added as she spotted the pastor approaching the door. "Here, let me take your coat and you can go into the drawing room with these two." *In addition, you can play referee*, she thought, although she refrained from voicing it aloud.

Kenneth smiled at her, and as Ethel and Lloyd preceded him into the drawing room, he said quietly, "I saw Florence and Ronald pulling in, and I notice you're acting nervous. Nervous is unlike you, Louise. Are Ethel and Florence having another tiff?"

"Not a tiff, exactly," she hedged, unwilling to involve her friend in a family concern. "It's just that the crafts fair has created some tensions."

"Ah. I see." He turned to enter the drawing room, then looked back at Louise and smiled. "I shall offer my services as a buffer, for what they are worth."

Everyone else arrived in short order, and Louise was kept busy introducing their two inn guests to the others. Ethel and Florence, thankfully, seemed busy chatting with other people and had not exchanged more than a "Happy Thanksgiving."

Several times, Louise glanced at her aunt, but Ethel was chatting in animated fashion with others at the table and seemed unconcerned that she had not spoken to Louise. Resentment and sadness churned in Louise's breast. She realized she had been too forceful with her suggestions and too abrupt in her criticism, but she had apologized. Ethel had made no effort to do anything of the sort, and yet she continued to behave as if Louise was the pariah. Once again, Louise wished Alice were here. Even if she could not do anything about their aunt's attitude, Louise would have welcomed the support.

Jane bustled back and forth, setting steaming bowls of vegetables on the table. Finally, she entered with the pièce de résistance, her marvelous turkey on a large platter, surrounded by greens and radishes for color. It had been carefully sliced so that the meat could easily be forked onto plates without disturbing the handsome effect.

"What a lovely meal you've prepared, Jane," said Ethel. "It's almost a shame to disturb it."

"Oh, wait! I have a digital camera," Florence said. "Let me take a picture before we sit down." She snapped several shots in short order, and then the guests took their places.

"This way, Alice will be able to see how our meal looked," said Ethel.

"After the meal, we could take a group picture," suggested Florence. "So you girls could show it to her when she returns."

"An excellent idea." Ethel beamed at Florence.

Louise could not help sliding a glance at Jane as Kenneth invited them all to bow their heads. Jane winked and grinned. It just went to show, Louise thought, that there was no predicting a person's behavior.

⟋

Thanksgiving at Camp Compassion was odd without her family, Alice decided. That was the only word for it. *Odd.*

The volunteers had set up two long tables end-to-end out in a grassy area. Along one side, a third table was placed to serve as a buffet. Riley had directed Miranda and Royce to cover the tables with sheets of white butcher paper with the shiny side up, for effect.

Diners were asked to bring their own chairs and drinks. Accordingly a variety of camp stools, lawn chairs and folding chairs were placed haphazardly, while water bottles, fruit juices and energy drinks dotted the tables.

Paper towels served as napkins, and there were paper plates and plastic utensils. But the meal itself was the most radical departure from that to which Alice was accustomed.

The meal had been provided by a vegetarian chef who volunteered his services and supplies after he'd read about the animal-rescue efforts online. The main dish, served in place of turkey, was butternut squash with whole-wheat, wild rice and onion stuffing. Alice knew the ingredients because on the buffet table where the food was set out, there were small placards indicating what each of the dishes was. There was something labeled a "Jerusalem Artichoke Salad." Baked maple-and-tarragon sweet potatoes, cranberry-apple sauce, and wine-and-honey-glazed brussels sprouts were among the other offerings. Finally, at the end of the table, to Alice's immense delight, was a familiar sight, pumpkin pie.

"This is amazing," Ellen said as they took their seats.

"Way beyond amazing, Mom." Miranda thanked her brother as he unfolded her stool for her. "How much cooler could it get than to have a vegetarian meal here?"

"I have to confess it never even occurred to me," June said. "I've been making turkey and stuffing for my kids, my brothers and their families for years. I guess I just assumed we'd have turkey."

"This is exciting." Alice picked up her fork and sniffed at the stuffing. "Yum."

Mark sat down on her other side, his own plate loaded with some of everything. "I'm starving."

She laughed.

Then Joe tapped on the end of the table. "All right, everybody. Someone said we need a prayer. But right now, around this table, there are people of at least three different faiths and probably more. I know this interesting fact because I asked."

There was a ripple of laughter around the table.

"So I'm going to keep it simple," Joe said. "Those of you who aren't believers, feel free to ignore us. I respect everyone's right to his or her own beliefs. Now, for those who wish to pray, let us bow our heads."

People began to clasp their neighbor's hands, although Joe had not suggested it. Heads bowed. Alice noted, just before she closed her eyes, that every single person at the table was participating.

"Dear God," Joe said, "we came here from different walks of life, from different faiths, different ethnicities, educations, careers and economic backgrounds. But we all came here because we believe. We believe we were called by You to care for Your creatures. We believe You are with us as we minister to animals in need. We believe Your hands guide us to find and heal them. We believe Your love flows through us when we share that love with them.

"We ask You to guide us to animals in need. We ask You to make healing instruments of our hands and help us stay strong despite the overwhelming scope of this disaster. We ask You to keep us safe as we travel long distances back to our homes, and we ask You to move the hearts of more people to join our efforts.

"Thank You, God, for each one of these very special people and for the bounty of this feast we share today. Thank You for families who understand why we can't be with them. Thank You for the camaraderie we share and the bonds that will hold us together forever from this day on. Thank You for all the lives we have saved through Your help. And keep those who didn't make it close in Your comforting embrace now, beyond pain and fear.

"In Your name we pray. Amen."

"Amen." A number of people around the table echoed the closing, but no one moved for a long moment. Finally Alice released Mark's and June's hands to pick up her paper towel and dab at her eyes. As she looked around, she saw that she was not the only one.

"Wow!" Seated beside Ellen, Kyle swiped the back of his arm across his eyes in a true too-manly-to-cry gesture. "Joe woulda made a good preacher."

"He said everything that was in my heart," Alice said quietly.

"Okay, folks," Joe called out, "our chef has gone way above and beyond the call with this meal. Dig in!"

Someone chuckled and they all began to eat.

⌒

Much later that evening, the trucks rolled in with more animals. Darrell and Oren had gone out, forgoing their own Thanksgiving, on another rescue mission. Alice was glad to know Joe had set heaping plates of food aside for them on their return.

Along with everyone else, Alice worked to get every frightened, starving animal documented and cared for as quickly as possible. Her final intake was a cat, and she sucked in her breath in dismay when she saw its condition.

Corinne shook her head as she handed Alice the towel-wrapped cat. It was completely limp, eyes open and pupils appearing fixed, and it had a huge open wound along one side of its head. The only sign of life was a thin, barely audible wheezing cry that accompanied the release of each shallow breath.

"This is not hurricane damage. This injury is recent," Alice said sadly. The cat was a gray-striped tabby that reminded her of Wendell right down to the four white stockings. She skipped any bathing and rushed it through intake straight to a vet exam. As luck—or lack of luck—

would have it, Mark was occupied and Dr. Spade was free. Alice took a deep breath, forcing herself to set aside her reluctance to experience any more of his cutting comments.

To her surprise, he thanked her as she set down her precious bundle. He gently unwrapped the towel and went over every inch of the unresponsive animal. After the examination, he straightened and shook his head. "I'm going to clean out this head wound. She has a broken jaw but there do not appear to be other broken bones or external injuries. The eyes and the lack of reflexes suggest to me that her brain is probably swelling." He ran a gentle hand down the cat's soft flank. "All we can do is hydrate her, keep her warm, and wait to see what happens."

"You mean she…could live?" Alice couldn't believe it.

Dr. Spade shrugged. "I wouldn't say her chances are good, but I've seen cats rebound from seemingly life-ending injuries before. There's a reason they say cats have nine lives. Let's not give up on her yet."

"Thank you." Alice laid the towel back over the kitty and slipped her hands beneath the floppy body, resolved to pray for the cat's survival for all she was worth.

"Alice?"

She glanced up. Dr. Spade had both hands flat on the table. He was gazing down at them. "I owe you an apology. I've been curt and unkind since I arrived and I'm sorry.

I drove straight down here from my father's funeral, and I've been exhausted. In retrospect, going from one emotional setting to another that is also overwhelming in a different way probably wasn't a good idea. But...I wanted to help."

"And you have."

He did not appear to register her words. "It's not an excuse, but I want you to know I'm not always...I'm not—"

"I understand." Alice stopped and regarded the man as he swallowed hard, compassion flooding her heart as she regretted her unkind thoughts about him. Grieving people handled their feelings in different ways. "Please accept my condolences. I lost my father not so long ago. I know how difficult it can be." She hesitated. "I'd be happy to add you to my daily prayer list."

Dr. Spade's head came up and he nodded, meeting her eyes for the first time since she had met him. "I would appreciate that. Thank you. And Alice?"

"Yes?"

"Please call me Luther."

She smiled again. "Of course."

"I noticed that you lead a Bible study group."

"Yes. Would you like to join us?"

He looked surprised. "Ah, no thank you. Not really my thing. But you might want to mention this cat to your group. She's going to need all the help she can get."

Alice nodded. "I've got that covered already." As she settled the little cat in a kennel with a heated rice bag beneath it, she reflected on the vet's change of attitude. *Thank You, Lord, for using me to help Dr. Spade through a difficult time. Help me always to be sensitive and kind in the face of anger and provocation. I can't see the suffering hidden behind a rough facade, but help me to practice compassion for all.* She glanced down at the little life in her hands. *And please, Lord, be with this kitty as she fights to live. Pour Your strength into her and heal her damaged body. In Your name I pray. Amen.*

Chapter Thirteen

*H*elp!"

Jane came unsteadily down the hall on the second floor, a tower of boxes stacked precariously in her arms.

Louise had just come out of the Sunset Room after placing fresh linens and towels in it for some new guests who would arrive later that day. She hurried forward and relieved her sister of the topmost two boxes. "What's this?"

"I'm moving all the raffle items from my room over to the Assembly Room," Jane said, panting a bit. "I'm so sorry I let Aunt Ethel maneuver me into this job."

"I'm not sorry," Louise told her. "You're doing wonderfully. If this succeeds, it's going to be thanks to you and all the work you've put into organizing the craft offerings."

"I am beginning to have a good feeling about it," Jane confessed as they entered the kitchen and set down their loads of boxes. "We've had a great response from vendors interested in renting booth space. As of this morning, I have the entire Assembly Room filled and a number of booths outside as well."

"What if we have rain or snow? That could be disastrous," Louise said.

The sides on the canopy that Aunt Ethel ordered can be lowered if the weather is bad," Jane explained. "Even if it rains, we should be okay. Snow, though, would be a different story. Of course, snow would be problematic in terms of drawing a crowd even if the whole thing were held inside." She shrugged. "Well, it won't do me any good to worry about something I have no control over. I'll continue to work on the things I can do to make this a success." She glanced at her watch. "Speaking of which, I have a meeting with Sylvia in forty-five minutes. I'd better get the car packed and get going."

After Jane left the kitchen, Louise sat down at the piano. She reached for the sheet music in the folder she had created for the Santa Lucia songs.

A moment later, Jane popped her head into the parlor. "Louise, I completely forgot. That honeymooning couple should be arriving sometime after two. I doubt I will be back by then. Will you mind registering them and showing them to the Sunset Room?"

"I'd be happy to." Louise was glad to take some pressure off her sister.

She ran through several sets of warm-up exercises so familiar that she did not even have to think about them. When she thought she was sufficiently prepared, she placed the first piece of music on the piano and opened it. She set her metronome to a stately pace and began to play. While she did not feel that she needed to have the pieces memorized, she wanted to have them firmly under her fingers so that she would be able to direct the children while she played. Muscle memory was a concept she introduced to her students at a young age in hopes that they would understand why it was so important to practice on a regular basis. The more one repeated an exercise or piece of music, the easier it became to flow from one section of music into the next.

The afternoon passed quickly. The young honeymooners, the Fergusons, arrived on time, and Louise showed them to their room. It was pleasant and satisfying to chat with the young couple. She shared the home's history and told them about growing up in the huge old Victorian home. She also shared the story of how she and her sisters had worked to make their vision of a bed-and-breakfast a reality. After getting them settled, she returned to her work.

She played for nearly two hours, keeping at it until she was satisfied that she had given her fingers plenty of exercise and her brain plenty of exposure to the music.

Before Alice went to work with Gina in the dog room, she stopped in the cat room. The room where they were keeping the very sick and injured cats was not much more than a large closet, but they didn't want to distress ailing felines by housing them with dogs who might bark.

It was Sunday, the morning of the third day since the little cat with the horrid head wound had been brought in. The first day she had battled for her life, lying unconscious, doing little more than taking shallow breaths. But yesterday morning, her eyes opened when someone spoke to her. She didn't eat, but toward nightfall, she lifted her head several times.

This morning, Alice could hardly believe her eyes. The little cat was on her feet. She was leaning drunkenly against the bars of the cage, but she was standing, an intravenous line trailing from one of her front legs.

"Isn't that terrific?" Gina said from the next kennel over, where she was washing down the steel walls with disinfectant. "She's trying. She even took a few sips of water this morning, although mostly she just dunked her face in the bowl. At noon, I'm going to try giving her a syringe of wet food."

"I can't believe it." Alice clapped three times in delight as the cat turned its head and stared at her with wide eyes. "Dr. Spade was right about her. I would never have believed this if I hadn't seen it."

"Don't get too excited," Gina cautioned. "I haven't seen her try to take a step yet. All manner of brain damage could be a problem. And I hate to break it to you, but I'm pretty sure she's blind."

Alice was stricken. "Are you sure?"

Gina nodded. She walked over to the cage. The cat turned its head and appeared to look at her, but when Gina waved a hand right in front of the bars and then poked a finger through, coming inches from its eyes, the cat never flinched or blinked.

"Oh no," Alice said in distress.

"Hey, there are worse things," Gina said. "I've seen a lot of blind cats and dogs, and honestly, they learn to get around extremely well. Besides, don't give up yet. She could regain some or even all of her vision."

Alice looked in at the cat. "I will never give up on you," she informed it, "and I will keep on praying because something sure seems to be working. Now I'd better get to work."

In the CCU, the shepherd stood when it saw her and poked its long muzzle as far through the bars of its kennel as possible. There was an empty bowl near the cage door. Alice couldn't help smiling as she saw it. She knelt and removed the bowl, taking a moment to fondle the shepherd's ears, happiness rushing through her.

The shepherd was doing better, eating by itself consistently, although it still looked dreadfully thin. Dr. Spade had told her the dog was one of the worst starvation cases he had ever seen.

Mark and Luther both were in the CCU, examining various dogs. When the little cocker spaniel with the tumor saw Alice, she began to do a delirious dance of joy, pawing at the bars. The tumor did not appear to cause her any pain.

The little dog had gotten more tolerant of other handlers, but it still was devoted to Alice and nearly went wild if she came in without greeting it.

"Gee, do you think she wants to go out?" Luther said. He was smiling, a change to which Alice still wasn't accustomed. To her surprise, his name tag today read "Luther."

She tapped it with one finger. "This is a nice change."

He looked sheepish. "I don't know why I didn't catch on to that earlier." He glanced at the cocker spaniel. "We would have had someone take her out, but we know she has a marked preference for you."

Mark chuckled. "Translation: None of us is eager to get a finger bitten off."

"Thanks for waiting, whatever your motives," Alice said, making both men grin. She got a lead and knelt before the cage. When the little dog came barreling out, she wriggled all over Alice's lap and licked her face.

"What's going to happen to her?" she asked the vets.

Luther's mouth compressed. "I don't know. None of the rescue groups will take her because of the medical costs and her probably limited life span."

Alice sighed. "She's been here a long time. I was beginning to wonder."

The vet nodded. "I don't suppose you want a sick dog that may not live long, do you?"

Alice grimaced. "My sisters would clobber me if I came home with a dog. And my cat might not be too thrilled either."

"Grace Chapel Inn is a busy place," Mark said. "It's probably not the best environment for this dog, anyway. She's not exceptionally friendly to most people, and you wouldn't want a guest to get bitten."

Alice's steps were heavy as they began their walk. Surely, someone had room in his or her heart for the little black-and-white dog.

Joe caught up with her as she and her cocker spaniel friend were heading back to the CCU after their walk.

"Alice? I need your input."

"My input?"

"Yes, in case there's anything I missed." He glanced down at his clipboard, which made Alice chuckle. Just yesterday, Royce and Miranda had hidden it as a practical joke. Joe was frantic until they confessed and retrieved it. "You're laughing at me again, running around with my notes. But these notes are what have kept this camp from becoming one huge, disorganized mess, you know."

"I do know and I appreciate it, Joe. We all do." She patted his arm. "Now, on what topic do you need my infinite wisdom?"

Joe grinned. "I wrote a set of protocols for volunteers to review when each helper arrives. It includes things like taking care of oneself by drinking plenty of water and getting enough rest, and other notes that are more directly related to animal care, particularly precautions when working with dogs. I think perhaps we should add that to the orientation." He shook his head. "We all expected that eventually someone would get bitten. But if you had told me it would be a Lab, I'd have laughed at the notion."

"I might have, too, before I got here," Alice said, "but all the animals are frightened and vulnerable, regardless of breed." She took the sheet of paper Joe handed her. "I'll look over this and see if I can think of anything you should add."

She returned to the CCU and put the cocker back in its kennel. She was standing by the exam table, looking over Joe's list, when she heard the door open. "Alice?"

It was Mark's voice. She looked up with a smile. "Hi."

"What's that?" He came and looked over her shoulder. "Ah, Joe's handiwork. I think it's an excellent idea. I guess no one thought of creating safety regulations sooner because we all were too busy. Hey." He pointed to number five on the list. "This clearly says, 'Do not skip meals.' You haven't eaten any lunch, have you?"

Alice looked at her watch and was surprised to see that it was past two o'clock. "No. I guess I forgot."

"You need to practice if you're going to preach," Mark said, grinning. He held up a brown bag that she hadn't noticed. "Two sandwiches. Do you have time to sit down and eat?"

Alice was warmed by his thoughtfulness and pleased that he had noticed her lapse. "I sure do. All our furry friends have been walked, and we've given midday meds, so barring any human emergencies, I can take a break."

She led the way into the room where the medical supplies were kept. The table was filled with all sorts of human and animal medications, but they took seats on one of the couches along the wall, placing the sandwiches in their laps. Mark also had brought along bottles of water, and she gratefully accepted one, knowing how easy it was to lose fluids even when it was not terribly hot. All of them at camp were doing hard physical labor, and many of them were office workers or people who spent their days in sedentary occupations. It was probably a miracle more of them hadn't collapsed.

As they unwrapped their sandwiches and began to eat, Alice said, "Do you feel the same? After having had this experience, I mean. Do you feel like the same person you were before you came down here?"

Mark stopped before he took another bite. He cocked his head, considering her question. "No," he said finally. "This has changed me—and the way in which I view the world—in a fundamental way."

"I believe that's true of me as well." Alice stared at her sandwich without really seeing it. "I will never hear about another natural disaster again without worrying about what happened to all the animals involved. But more than that, I've learned things about myself."

"Such as?"

"I'm a lot more capable than I thought I was. I wasn't sure I would be much help with animals, although I felt certain I should be doing this. Also, I've learned that I can feel heartache and discouragement and all manner of other disappointment without losing my belief that God is at work in the world. I've learned that there are more people who care deeply about animals than I've ever dreamed of, and that we can make positive strides in animal care and treatment if we work together."

Mark was smiling. "You sound like you've become quite an animal advocate."

"It's going to be hard to go home tomorrow." She set down her sandwich, suddenly not hungry anymore.

"Hey." Mark settled a comforting arm around her shoulders. "Don't—"

A fist appeared through the open doorway and knocked on the frame. It belonged to one of the volunteers who had arrived just that morning. "Sorry to interrupt a married moment but Corinne needs you, Alice."

"Oh, we're not married," both Mark and Alice said together.

"Just old friends," Alice added quickly.

"But very good old friends," Mark said.

Alice turned as she was leaving the room and shook an admonishing finger at him for teasing her, and he grinned and winked.

Corinne was waiting on the grass in front of the house. A blond man stood beside her, twisting a ball cap in his big hands. He looked to be roughly Jane's age, and as she neared, Alice could see that his hair was highlighted by strands of gray.

"Hello," she said. "I'm Alice."

"This is Tom," Corinne said. "He's looking for his dog."

"I've been to a bunch of the rescue places," the man said. "Nobody had a dog like my Whitley." At the last word, his voice broke. "Sorry," he muttered.

Alice felt a rush of sympathy. Every day desperate people came through the camp, seeking their pets. Twice the volunteers had witnessed joyous reunions, but far more frequent were these devastating, disappointing moments. All the camp team could do was direct such people to any other rescue centers they might not have visited yet.

"I had to go over and get my mother to evacuate, so I left Whitley in the house with the dog door open like I always do when I leave so he could come and go," Tom told her. "And after I picked up Ma I went back, but the highway patrol wouldn't let me go that way. They made me turn 'round and drive inland. Said the storm was coming any minute. I had to go."

He lowered his head, mangling the hat in his hands even more. "All I could think about was how afraid he was and how I promised him I'd be back for him. He trusted me and I let him down."

Several other volunteers had gathered around as Tom told his story and like Alice, they all had tears in their eyes by now. Alice stood quietly, letting him grieve although she did not understand why Corinne had asked for her.

"Alice." Corinne's eyes were intent. "Whitley is a male German shepherd."

"I looked," Tom said, "and you all have four shepherds, but none of them were my guy. Thanks for trying though."

Alice barely heard the end of his sentence. She turned and ran back to the house as Corinne said, "We have one more shepherd here, Tom. He was really sick but..."

In the CCU, Alice's hands were shaking so badly that she could barely get a slip lead over the shepherd's head. "Oh, please be Whitley," she said to the dog.

The dog's big ears went straight up.

Alice's heart stuttered for a moment. "Whitley," she said again.

The shepherd cocked his head and whined, his eyes bright and alert. And Alice knew.

She walked out the door of the house with the shepherd, trying to contain her hope. The odds were slim, she told herself, even if the dog had seemed to respond to the name. It wasn't wise to get too excited.

Tom was with Corinne on the far side of the yard, his eyes glued on the house. As Alice and the dog appeared, both hands flew out in entreaty. "Whitley!" he called as he dropped to his knees, his face and voice joyous.

Alice released the dog's leash as he surged forward with a surprising amount of energy and dashed across the yard. He bowled into Tom, who threw his arms around the dog. Licking his face, Whitley pranced and bounced so wildly that he knocked his owner completely onto the ground, where the two rolled around as Tom rubbed the broad head, stroked the long nose and ran his hands over every inch of the big-boned frame.

"He's so thin," he said, his voice breaking as he buried his face in his dog's thick coat.

"He looks better now than he did when he came in," Alice told the man. "He's been eating well recently."

Finally, Tom raised his head. Tears were unashamedly streaming down his tanned cheeks. "Thank you," he said, choking on the words. "I can never thank you enough."

"Thank Alice," Luther said. "If she hadn't spent hours coaxing Whitley to eat, your dog wouldn't be here today. He was in really bad shape when he came in."

The words warmed Alice. She realized through her tears that practically the whole camp had gathered around them. People were videotaping, snapping pictures, grinning and hugging each other. Tom stepped forward and hugged her, and Whitley leaped up on his powerful haunches to join them.

"Group hug!" someone called, laughing.

Joe bounded onto the hood of a nearby truck. "This!" he yelled, pointing at Tom and his dog. "This—right here— is why you came down here, people. This is what makes it worth the work."

Alice flashed back to the night the dog had been brought in, lying on the rotting board, barely alive. It had, indeed, been worth it. "Thank You, Lord," she whispered.

"I want to pay you." Tom got to his feet. Whitley huddled his big body as close to Tom's legs as he could get and the man kept one hand on his dog's big head as he reached into his hip pocket. "I don't have much," he began, but Joe shook his head.

"You told me you lost everything. Use it for him," he said, pointing to the dog, "and for your family. The one thing we'd like you to do is spread the word. Spread the word to other people searching for their pets, spread the word to others who are in a position to send donations, and spread the word to people willing to come and work with us."

Tom nodded. He bent and cupped his dog's face in his hands, laughing as Whitley licked him squarely across the chin. "You hear that, big guy? We have to spread the word."

Chapter Fourteen

*L*ouise and Karin planned a second rehearsal of the Santa Lucia celebration for Sunday afternoon. All the children indicated they could attend, so even though she hated to interrupt family time on Sundays, Louise scheduled the rehearsal.

The Lindars family was waiting at the church for Louise at three on Sunday. "Good afternoon, Mrs. Smith," the children chorused as they piled out of the family van.

"Good afternoon." Louise straightened the collar of her ivory sweater as she removed her coat. She had changed her clothing after church, not wanting to appear too dressed up. Working with young people was a balancing act between appearing authoritative and not appearing so fuddy-duddy that they tuned one out, she had learned. She looked around expectantly. "Where is your mother?"

"She's got the flu." Mattias, the nine-year-old, scrunched up his face comically. "She looks gross."

"Mattie, hush." Marit, his fourteen-year-old sister who would be the Lucia in the service, stepped in front of her wayward sibling and shooed him out of the way. Louise saw that Mr. Lindars had gotten out of the van as well.

"Karin says to tell you she's so sorry she can't be here," Kettil Lindars said. "She sent this." He extended a folder toward Louise. "Here is the costume information you can share with the group. She says there is a recipe in there, too, if your sister would like to look at it."

Louise took the folder automatically. "But…your wife seemed fine at church this morning."

"I know," he said, shrugging. "Mattie had it last week. It comes on suddenly. We're hoping no one else catches it. Luckily, it only lasts about a day, so she should be here for the next rehearsal."

Louise sighed. "Please tell her I hope she feels better soon."

"Will do. Thank you, Mrs. Smith." Mr. Lindars jumped back into his van and pulled away.

As Louise entered the chapel, she muttered, "I *really* hope she feels better soon."

Louise pulled the piano from its niche near the altar and took the dust cover off it. The piano was regularly tuned for events such as Bible school and special programs like this one.

She adjusted the stool to the proper height for her, then spread out her music neatly across the piano and opened Karin's folder. Before rehearsal began, she had asked several of the parents to attend a brief costuming committee meeting. Karin was supposed to speak about what the participants might wear. Quickly, she looked over the notes so that she would be able to share the correct information.

She had planned on getting started promptly with the children, but now she would need to take time for this costuming pow-wow first. With so few rehearsals, they needed every moment to prepare their music. She intended to rehearse the songs the children already knew, then add another. She also hoped to have time to show all the children how the Lucia procession would line up.

"Mama sent some pictures from my old church of what our costumes looked like." Marit noticed the sign-up sheets Louise had laid on a nearby table. "Would you like me to put them out with the sign-ups?"

"Yes. Thank you, dear. That would be very helpful."

The chapel door opened and a swarm of children and a few adults came drifting in along with a whiff of the crisp autumn air. Louise glanced at her watch and then nodded approvingly as the first children took their seats.

⟳

The Camp Compassion Bible group met that afternoon. Alice had been worrying silently for several days about who would carry on in her absence.

Their little group had swelled to a dozen people over the past week. Faces came and went according to who arrived, who left and who had chores to do on any given day, but the group persisted. Alice felt that they had provided each other with much-needed spiritual support.

"Today I thought we could read a passage from the fourth chapter of 1 Peter. It's about recognizing our own special gifts and abilities. I thought it might be appropriate, since many of us really had no idea we could be so helpful before coming down here," she said to the group. "But before we begin, I have to bring up a matter of concern." She paused, looking around at the faces of these strangers who had become comrades both in their work and in their spiritual quest. "Ellen, Royce and Miranda left us this morning. June and I are leaving tomorrow. I would ask that as we pray and study here together, all of you search your hearts and ask God if He is calling you to step forward and assume the leadership of the group. You need no prior experience. With your willingness, the Holy Spirit will guide your words."

A man seated at the far side of the rough circle they had assumed raised a hand. "Alice, my name is Sherman. I only have been here for two days, but I would be happy to lead the group while I'm here. Perhaps before I leave, someone else will feel the call."

Alice blinked. Could it really be that easy? "Thank you, Sherman," she said warmly. "Your willingness to lead eases my concern about leaving." *And thank You, Lord, for Your all-knowing presence in our lives. I should have given this to You days ago instead of worrying about it on my own.*

⌒

Jane was at the registration desk when she heard the rattle of the back door not long before dinner. She had just finished taking a reservation for January.

"Louise? I'm in here. Hey, I had this great idea for a Valentine's Day promotion. I think we could fill all—"

Her sister's appearance in the foyer stopped her in midsentence.

"Louise! What happened to you?"

Her eldest sister, normally the calm and unflappable one, looked as if she had been thoroughly shaken up. Her eyes were a bit glassy and her carefully coiffed silver hair was slightly mussed—something that Jane rarely saw. The skirt and sweater that had looked so crisp and attractive when she had left for rehearsal was wilted.

"I," she said precisely, "have had an unutterably miserable forty-five minutes."

"What happened?"

"The first problem was that Karin Lindars apparently got the flu right after church," Louise recounted mournfully. "She was supposed to meet with the parents to discuss costumes while I began rehearsals, but since she was ill I had to do it. That meant that the children had to wait for almost fifteen minutes."

"Unsupervised?"

"Yes. Well, I was in the room and so were a number of parents, but the children were getting fidgety and silly. When I finally began rehearsal, Delissa Anderstrand would not speak her lines."

"Who's...Melissa Anderstrand?"

"De-lissa," Louise corrected. "She's in kindergarten. She is extremely shy and just stood there looking blank each time she had a line, but that was not such an issue. I'll just have another child ready to step in if she can't do it. Then I turned around and Kate Waller's little sister was sobbing her heart out. It took me ten minutes to figure out what was wrong."

"Was she hurt?"

"Wha...? Oh no." Louise flapped a hand as if to wave away that suggestion. "She was crying because Tiffany Sherman got a speaking part and she did not. Apparently the two girls are friends and occasional rivals. Now how was I to know that?" she demanded in an aggrieved tone. "They didn't write that down on their information sheets at the first session!"

Jane bit her lip so she would not smile. "No, I guess they wouldn't have."

"So I decided to split the part between them. It was a large part, anyhow. Tiffany wasn't very happy, of course, but the problem was solved." She fell silent for a moment.

Jane couldn't stand it. "And then what happened?"

Louise sniffed. "Morley Trimble happened, that's what. He told me at the beginning of the rehearsal that his tummy hurt, but you know how children can be. Aches and pains always crop up when they're asked to do something they don't enjoy."

"You didn't believe him?"

"I'm afraid not." Louise lifted her head and slowly let out a breath. "I urged him to sit down and sing with us. Which he did. Until halfway through the rehearsal. All of a sudden, Morley jumped up and ran out of the room. I saw that he was headed for the restroom and deduced that he had not been pretending about feeling ill, so I sent an older boy to see if he was all right. As he left, he tripped over Delissa's foot and fell. I saw him going down and attempted to catch him."

"Attempted?"

"Attempted. I was not successful, but my less than graceful swan dive provided the children with quite a bit of amusement. Needless to say, my rehearsal effectively ended at that point."

"Who knew a music rehearsal could be so traumatic?"

Louise looked at her sharply as if she suspected Jane was laughing at her. Jane managed to keep a perfectly straight face…for a moment. But she couldn't contain herself, and she had to chuckle as she came out from behind the desk and patted Louise's shoulder. "Why don't you come into the kitchen, and I'll cut you a nice slice of chocolate cake?"

Louise sighed. "I'm not sure that even chocolate can make me feel better after that rehearsal."

∽

It could not be Monday morning already, could it?

Alice walked across the grass with June, looking around as if she wanted to memorize every moment.

"I can't believe we have to leave," June said. "How did two weeks fly by so fast?"

"I don't know. I'm not ready to go either. They still need help."

"Joe said there was a new team from Ohio coming in today," June reminded her. "And I imagine they'll get a few more like us, who didn't ask but just decided to come down and help. We have to trust God on this one, Alice. He'll provide."

"You're right. I've prayed about it." They all had. Several days before, their Bible group meeting had focused on asking the Lord for what was needed. "What time do you want to pull out?" she asked June. "Do I have time to help with breakfast feeding?"

"Oh, sure. I thought if we got on the road around nine we'd be doing fine. Would it be okay with you if we stop overnight this time? I'm just too tired to drive straight through, even taking turns."

"That's wise." Alice forced herself to think of the pleasures of going home rather than the heartaches of leaving. "We aren't going to know how to act when we can get real showers and sleep in real beds."

"Well, I guess I'll work with Jules one last time," June said, naming the woman in charge of the room where the well cats were housed. "Shall we meet back here at eight forty-five?"

"All right. I'm going to the CCU. See you in a little while."

It was nearly seven already. She had said good-bye to Mark, a parting that had ended with a tender hug between them. Her spirits had been lifted, but now she felt sad about leaving all her furry charges. She stopped in the cat room to see how "her" kitty was doing.

Alice's heart sank when she saw that the little cat with the head wound wasn't in her cage. Had she taken a turn for the worse during the night?

"What happened to our wounded kitty?" she asked as Gina appeared in the doorway leading to the dog room.

"Oh, don't panic. She's fine," said Gina hastily. "Sorry to give you such a scare. Luther took her into the meds room because that's the only quiet place in the whole joint and he wanted to evaluate her a little bit."

Alice couldn't resist. She slipped into the meds room, closing the door behind her. "Do you mind if I watch?"

Luther was on the floor with the cat. "Not at all."

The cat had heard Alice's voice and came stepping daintily toward her. There was a table leg in the way and Alice sucked in a breath of dismay as the cat headed straight for it. But at the last minute, it slowed and cautiously moved around the leg. It walked in an odd little circle to the right before straightening itself out and coming closer.

"Did you see that? She can walk. And I think she can see."

Luther nodded. "I think you're right. She has some sight—not much, but some—and that may improve as her brain heals. We'll just have to wait. The circling also is brain damage. But given the blow she must have taken to the head, just having her on her feet moving around is a victory."

"I'm so glad." She hesitated for a moment. "Will the circling go away?"

"It may or it may not. If it doesn't, it still might lessen. Either way, it doesn't necessarily mean she can't have a good quality of life. I have a brain-damaged cat at home, and he gets around just fine. We'll just have to watch her for the next few weeks."

Alice marveled to herself at the change in the veterinarian since the day she first met him. She supposed that since he was a vet, she should have expected him to own pets, but the thought really never crossed her mind.

"I'm leaving today," she told him.

"You are? That's unfortunate. I suppose since you've been here so long, I assumed you were permanent. But now I remember Mark mentioned something about your owning an inn."

"Part of me wishes I were staying," Alice confessed, "but the other part is eager to get home. I miss my family and the inn."

Luther's expression sobered and she remembered that he had lost his father recently. "Yes, I'm going to my sister's house after I leave here, and I feel the same way."

Alice hesitated. "I have a question for you."

"If I can answer it, I will."

"What would you think if I were to take the cocker spaniel with me? Not to keep forever, but I could take her into foster care until I can find the right someone for her. My friend June—you know, June from the cat room—knows a vet at home who might treat her for free if you think she's healthy enough to travel." By the time she finished, she was rushing through her speech.

Luther's eyebrows rose. "You know you need Joe's permission, not mine or Mark's, to take a dog."

She nodded. "I can't keep her. I already have a cat. I want your opinion on her health. I value Mark's opinion, too, but since he knows me personally, I wanted to get someone else's thoughts on the matter."

"My thoughts on the matter...I think that dog would love to go home with you, Alice, and Joe will be thrilled to let you take her. I think a vet with the proper equipment needs to take a thorough look at that mass. It does look malignant, but you never know until you biopsy it, which we cannot do here. And even if it is malignant, if it is contained and hasn't spread to organs, she might have a chance. However, you have to face the fact that you could be dealing with a terminally ill animal that might not have a lot of time left. What will you do then?"

"I've thought about that," she told him, although her voice quivered at the mere thought of the little dog's dying. "If her life expectancy is brief, I'll keep her. She deserves to be comfortable and loved after all she's been through."

Luther nodded. "Then I think you should take her."

"Thank you." Alice beamed. She bent and stroked the cat, which had settled down at her feet and was placidly washing herself. "Get well, little one. I hope you find your family or a wonderful home."

Joe laughed when she asked him about taking the cocker. "I planned on it," he said, showing her a chart on which he already had written her name. "I knew you'd never be able to leave that little dog behind."

June's eyebrows almost merged with her blonde hair when Alice asked her how she would feel about taking the dog along. "Of course. That's fabulous, Alice. Once we get back to civilization and my cell phone works, I'll call my vet and explain the situation. Before I came down here, he told me that he would donate the initial treatment fees for any animal I brought home." She grinned. "And besides, I sort of forgot to tell you we're also taking the two tiger kittens whose mother died."

"June!" Alice was laughing. "We'll never be allowed to go away again, you realize?"

⌒

They arrived that evening at a modest motel along the interstate in Virginia just above the North Carolina border. While both women were longing for hot showers and soft mattresses, they felt it would not be ethical to sneak the animals in as several of their fellow volunteers had told them to do, so Alice went inside to speak to the desk clerk. If the motel wouldn't let them have the animals in their room, perhaps the SUV could be parked near the back of the lot and the two women could sleep there with their pets.

"Hello. I would like a room for two," Alice said in response to the pleasant-voiced brunette who was manning the desk. "However, we have a special situation."

"Oh?" The woman cocked her head.

"We are returning from a camp in Florida where we worked with an animal-rescue group for the past two weeks. We have a small dog and two cats—all in kennels—traveling with us. These pets will be placed in foster care while we try to locate families for them." Alice sucked in a breath, prepared to plead her case.

"Oh, honey, that is so sweet. You folks all are angels." To Alice's relief, the woman began to nod. "We'll make a special exception for you, even though we normally only allow service animals. I have a room right next to the east exit. It's a big room with plenty of space for your babies, and there's a grassy area yonder where you can take them to potty. Just please take a bag and clean up after them."

"Thank you so much." Alice pulled out her credit card. "You have no idea how much I appreciate your kindness. This trip has introduced me to so many extraordinary people with huge hearts." She finished her transaction and received key cards for herself and June.

"Once you get them settled, we'd love to see them if they're calm enough," the woman said. "But we understand if they're too traumatized. If I'd been able to take time away, I'd have gone down there too. It just broke my heart seeing all those animals on TV, so scared and hungry."

Alice thought of Whitley, the shepherd who nearly hadn't made it. "It was heartbreaking in some ways," she agreed. "But I felt that we really made a difference. I wish you could have seen how many people came. I never would have imagined there were so many people willing to sacrifice their vacation time or their sick pay. There were volunteers from all over the country."

The woman's eyes were shining. "I don't have any more leave until the start of the new year, or I'd love to do that."

"Oh, you could," Alice assured her. "They are going to need help down there for a very long time. Months, I'm sure. Here." She picked up one of the pens at the registration desk, and the woman handed her a piece of paper torn from a hotel notepad. "This is the Web site address for Camp Compassion, the place where I worked. They are trying to get information out regularly, but right now news has to be driven to an open post office and sent to the lady who handles the site. The man in charge at the camp is Joe MacAfell, and this is his cell phone number. There's no service out at the camp right now, but I hope there will be soon. If you're serious, Joe would love to have you go on down."

"What could I do? I love animals but I don't know all that much about taking care of them."

Alice laughed. "That's exactly how I felt before I went. Don't worry. If you have two hands, they will find work for you. I walked and fed dogs, cleaned cages and helped give medications. My friend June did a lot of laundry and helped in the cat room."

She spoke with the woman a bit more, sharing information about the experience. As she walked back out to the car to direct June to their room, it occurred to her that she just had done exactly what Joe wanted: She had spread the word and gotten someone else to consider volunteering. She was the new Shelby! The thought made her chuckle as she hopped back into the passenger seat and waved the key cards at June. "They were delighted to help, and all five of us have a room."

"Woo-hoo!" June let out a whoop that must have startled Alice's cocker, because there was a short, sharp yip from the kennel in the back. "God is good!"

Chapter Fifteen

As they approached Acorn Hill, both Alice and June grew quiet. The town looked the same as it had when they left . . . so how could they feel so changed?

As they drove along Acorn Avenue, Alice murmured, "I feel so different."

"We are different. We have met people with the same commitment to animals that we have, people willing to step outside their comfort zones, people from diverse backgrounds."

Alice glanced at her watch. "It's almost time for the evening feeding back at the camp."

"I would be finishing laundry and then going in to help Jules bottle-feed those kittens who came in orphaned on Friday."

"And I'd be in the CCU with Gina. Did you see the little black terrier that came in last night?"

"The one with the leg that looked—"

"Broken. It was. Luther stabilized it. He planned to splint it today. I hope that went all right."

There was a silence in the vehicle. Alice suspected June was feeling the same reluctance she was to step back into the "real" world. Knowing they probably would never see most, if any, of their fellow camp volunteers again created a stunning sense of loss.

"The worst part," said June, "is that we can't even call them for an update." She put on her turn signal and deftly veered into the driveway at the left side of the inn.

Home.

An immense sense of peace stole over Alice despite her sadness. Oh, she was going to miss everyone at camp, but she could not wait to see her sisters again!

June did not drive into the parking lot. Instead, she stopped beside the walk that led to the back door. They had so many things to unload that it would be silly to take any more steps than they had to.

Alice pressed her hands together, thinking about the canine guest her sisters soon would be meeting. She hoped Louise would not be too upset. Alice could count on Jane's heart to melt once she laid eyes on the cocker spaniel, but Louise was wooed less easily. She would have things to say about dog hair on the furniture, making sure the dog didn't bite anyone, and keeping the dog out of the kitchen...all eminently practical things that would make a great deal of sense, things with which Alice could agree.

However, with the new perspective Alice had acquired, a little dog hair did not seem like such a big deal.

Wendell was a different story. Alice bit her lip. The family feline was cuddly and affectionate, and she hoped that would not change with the introduction of the new animal. There simply was not a good way to explain to their cat that the dog was only a temporary addition to the household.

"Alice! You're home!" The back door flew open and Jane appeared at the rear of the inn.

Louise was right behind her. "Hello, dear. Oh, we have missed you. Thanksgiving just wasn't the same."

"Nor was it for us." Alice spoke into Louise's shoulder as her older sister pulled her into a surprisingly fierce hug.

"My turn," Jane proclaimed as her sisters parted. "We're so glad you're back."

"You just want me to get back to work, don't you?" Alice teased. As Jane released her, she walked to the back of the SUV, where June was just opening the doors.

Her sisters both greeted June warmly.

"What can we do?" Jane asked. "Load us up."

Alice and June glanced at each other.

"Uh-oh." Louise was astute at reading body language. "What was that look for?"

"What look?" Alice was sure she had not "looked" any particular way.

Jane ducked behind Alice. "Oh my goodness!"

"What?" Louise looked somewhat alarmed.

Alice laid a hand on her arm. "We have a short-term guest."

"A guest?"

"All of them?" Jane had seen the cats too.

"No." Alice smiled at Louise. "I promise you right here, right now, that this is a temporary situation. I brought home a dog."

"A dog."

Alice nodded. "It's a female, a small female." June had opened the cocker's kennel and slipped a lead over the dog's head. It jumped down, shaking itself vigorously. The moment it stopped, it made a beeline for the grass beside the gravel.

"She's housebroken," Alice said weakly.

"Indeed." Louise quirked an eyebrow up. "And how do you think Wendell is going to like her?"

"I don't know," Alice admitted. "But it will be very short-term, just until I find the right foster home, and I probably can keep them separated if I have to."

"It's a girl?" Jane knelt in the driveway. "Hello, pretty girl. How are you?"

"She may not like—"

But the warning Alice had been about to deliver was unheeded as Jane reached out and stroked the dog's soft head and ears without incurring so much as a lift of the lip. Alice and June both stared.

"Well," said Louise, "she is rather pretty. Tell us her story." As she spoke, she too knelt and stroked the cocker spaniel. Alice was dumbstruck by the sight of her proper sister Louise kneeling to pet a dog.

"She came in our very first night at Camp Compassion," June began. "And she—Alice, will you look at that?"

The dog rolled over on its back, inviting Louise to pat its belly. The position exposed the ugly tumor for all to see.

"Goodness, what is that?" Louise asked, her hand never faltering as she patted the little dog's belly up above the affected area. It was exactly the way Alice petted her little friend.

"Oh no. Is that a tumor, Alice?" Jane looked stricken.

"It is." Alice said reluctantly. She had not anticipated both her sisters actually liking the dog, and she hated to tell them that the cocker spaniel's life probably was limited. "It's why I brought her. No one else wanted her. She was there two whole weeks," she added indignantly. "Other cute, small dogs were taken by rescue groups but no one would take her once they learned she was ill."

"What's her prognosis?" Louise turned to look up at Alice.

"I don't know," Alice admitted. "Mark and the other vet, Luther Spade, think it looks malignant, but there was no way to biopsy it. June says her vet will donate some of her care."

"You should have seen her down there." June jumped in to bolster Alice's explanation. "She adored Alice. No one else could even pet her without getting growled at."

Jane and Louise both looked back down at the dog, lying on her back with her legs splayed, tongue hanging out, the picture of doggie contentment. "This dog?" they said in unison.

June and Alice both laughed. "This dog," June said.

"You said this is a temporary situation," Jane said suddenly. "Do you think you'll have to …?"

"No. At least I hope not," said Alice. "What I meant was that she would stay with us only until I can find a good foster home for her."

"A few days? A few weeks?" Louise was still patting the dog's belly.

"Either. It simply depends on how long it takes the right person to step forward. I've been praying about it."

"We will too," Jane assured her. "Does she have a name?"

Alice shook her head. "I wasn't sure if I should name her."

"Well, she can't just go around nameless," Louise said. "It could be some time before we find her a foster home or her own family is located."

"Alice, you're the one who saved her. You should name her," June said as she began to pull Alice's things out of the back of the SUV.

"But I can't think of anything interesting or original," Alice protested.

"Traveler," Jane said. "That's exactly what she's been doing."

"That's not a name for a pretty little female," Louise protested. "How about something like Amanda or Heather?"

Jane rolled her eyes. "Ick! Maybe Cinder or Soot, since she's got a lot of black on her?"

"No," said Alice, "I've got it."

Both her sisters stopped and looked at her.

"Miracle. Because she is." Alice was near tears. "If you had seen the shape many of these animals were in when they arrived, you'd know just how miraculous it is that she's doing so well."

"Miracle. I think it's perfect." Jane rubbed a hand up and down Alice's back in a comforting gesture.

The sisters made short work of unloading Alice's supplies from the SUV. When that was done, they met June's kittens, and finally they exchanged hugs and thanks with June before she drove home.

Alice set up the kennel in the corner of the kitchen. Miracle was sniffing happily along the cabinets beneath the kitchen counter, searching for crumbs, Alice supposed, when she heard Jane give a small gasp.

Alice turned to see Wendell poised in the doorway.

All three sisters froze. Wendell's tail puffed up right before their eyes.

Miracle turned and saw the cat, and Alice braced herself for a quick intervention if the dog tried to chase Wendell. But to her astonishment, Miracle only stared at the cat for a long moment, then broke the eye contact and went back to snuffling around the kitchen.

Wendell advanced with a stiff-legged stride that would have been amusing if Alice hadn't been so tense. He stopped a scant foot from the dog. Miracle turned and stared. She gave an experimental little yip and Wendell hissed. Miracle took a step back, appeared to shrug off the threat, and with a happy little bounce, lay down and rolled over onto her back. She wriggled this way and that before flipping to her stomach and resting her head on her paws, watching the cat.

Wendell simply looked down his nose at this display of canine idiocy. Then, as all three sisters stared, he stepped forward and butted his head against the dog, turning to rub across the dog's nose with his shoulder and flank.

Alice drew in a breath. "Thank the Lord," she murmured.

"Pardon?" Louise moved her gaze from the animals and looked at Alice.

"I've been so worried about how you all might feel about me bringing home a dog that could become quite ill, and I've worried about how Wendell would react."

"Wendell," said Jane succinctly, "is still the king of this roost."

The sisters chuckled as they turned their attention to the things that Alice had brought back. Most items were taken straight to the laundry room. Louise hung the sleeping bag over the porch rail to air out for a few hours while Jane began emptying the large cooler Alice had taken on the trip.

"You won't believe all the things I've received for the crafts fair," she told Alice. "In the two weeks you were gone, my room began to look like I was holding the craft show there. We moved everything over to the Assembly Room for storage just about the time I thought I was going to have to sleep in your bed for a while."

"Gracious! That sounds like a lot."

"You will not believe it until you see it for yourself," said Louise. "Jane, Sylvia and Florence succeeded beyond anything Aunt Ethel could have dreamed."

"Is there going to be room for everything? The Assembly Room doesn't sound large enough."

"Aunt Ethel decided that the Assembly Room was too limited a space. She talked a wedding planner over in Potterston into providing a tent by giving them a booth at no cost to display their services. Then she was worried that it might be too cold outside, so she has vendors coming to sell hot chocolate, apple cider, hot dogs and funnel cakes. One man has a cider press demonstration that people can try. A woman is going to demonstrate carding and spinning raw wool, and the 4-H Club is coming to talk to the crowd about the puppies they are raising to become guide dogs."

Alice shook her head. "I knew when I first heard her talk about the idea that this crafts fair was going to be more than just a small, beginner's attempt. She doesn't do anything halfway," she said fondly.

Louise was pointedly silent, and Alice remembered the tiff between her sister and their aunt. She was getting surprisingly tired, considering that she had slept well in the motel the night before and had done nothing but drive or ride for the past day.

"How is your Advent service coming, Louise?" she asked, trying not to yawn.

"It's not for Advent," Louise reminded her. "It's a new undertaking in honor of a saint named Lucia, or Lucy. She was a Christian martyr."

Louise went on at length to explain about Lucia and her crown of lights, and about the procession, which would involve handmaidens, and something called star boys. She recited the words of each of the songs she had found and was teaching the children.

"And they have special foods that I'm going to help with," Jane added.

By now, Alice was so tired she was having trouble following the conversation. When Jane asked if she would like to go upstairs and see some craft donations that had yet to be sent to the Assembly Room, Alice felt forced to shake her head. "My heart is willing but I am exhausted," she said. "Would you two mind if I went to lie down for an hour or so until dinner?"

Jane and Louise both stared at her for a moment. Then Jane quickly said, "Of course not, Alice. I imagine you must be beat after all that work and travel."

Perhaps it was Alice's imagination, but she was afraid she could read hurt feelings in her sisters' reactions. But for once in her life, Alice did not have the energy to try to smooth things out.

She dragged up the stairs to her room and slowly slipped off her outer clothing. Then she donned a light robe and moved onto her bed. She stared at the ceiling for a few moments. *Lord, please watch over my friends who are still at camp. Let them be joined by new volunteers, and let them find every animal in need.*

Alice looked around her room, seeing but not seeing the familiar yellow room with its soft pastels. Her heart still was at Camp Compassion. She wondered what her sisters would say if she told them that she wished she could return.

⌒

"How are you feeling?" Jane looked at Alice strangely on Wednesday morning when she came down for breakfast. "You were so quiet at dinner last night, but Louise and I assumed you were just exhausted from your drive."

"Not just the drive. We worked from before sunup until well after dark every day." She ran a hand down the neat polo shirt she wore with her jeans. "It feels odd not to be wearing a T-shirt."

"I took Miracle outside for a bit and fed her. She's asleep now, poor thing. She must be exhausted too."

"Well, then I'll leave her alone. Thank you for tending to her."

"My pleasure." Pouring the batter for waffles onto the hot waffle iron, Jane glanced at the time. "So what would you be doing now?"

Alice took a deep sniff. Chocolate chip waffles were one of her sister's specialties and normally Alice adored them. This morning, they smelled as wonderful as they always did, but Alice found she was not hungry. "It's a little after eight. Let's see... I would be finished feeding the dogs in the critical care unit, and Gina, my friend who is a vet tech, would be giving medications. I usually checked the intravenous bags for the animals on fluids. Then we would start walking them all, one at a time. As we returned with each animal, we marked the daily chart on the front of their cage for regularity, as well as for meals and meds. It was like being in a ward with more than a dozen patients at once, in a way. I didn't have much time to stop and reflect."

"I guess not." Jane flipped the waffles out of the iron and poured in more batter. She slid the plate on which she'd placed the finished waffles into the oven to keep them warm.

Alice went on to provide a thorough overview of life at Camp Compassion.

Jane regarded her with sympathy. "You're really missing it, aren't you?"

Alice nodded. "It's hard to explain. This is my life, but that was my life, too, for a very intense, short period of time, and it feels as if part of me has been ripped away. I know I can't go back, and yet that is all I have thought about since I got home. I've never felt so needed in my entire life."

"But you're a nurse. Haven't there been many times when someone would have died or suffered without your direct care?"

"Yes, but it's just not the same." Alice slumped in her seat. "I can't explain it."

"You don't have to." Jane left the stove long enough to bend down and hug Alice. "I can see how conflicted you are. What do you plan to do today?"

"First of all, I want to call the vet and make an appointment for Miracle. I also want to call my supervisor and let her know I'm back and able to work whenever she needs me. I thought I'd help you around here, and then this evening I have a meeting with the ANGELs. I'm eager to see what they have done with the bracelet project in my absence."

Louise came into the kitchen just in time to hear the end of Alice's speech. She wore a gray-blue twin set today and her pearls gleamed against the soft color. "Oh dear!" she said. "I was hoping you would go along with me to my Lucia rehearsal this evening."

"I'm sorry," Alice said, "but Britt Nilsen already planned this meeting and I can't miss it. I have been away from them long enough already."

Louise looked at Jane.

"Don't look at me for help." Jane waved a batter-covered spatula at her eldest sister. "Sylvia's coming over this evening so we can go over all the craft contributions and identify the people we still need to gather things from. Besides, your rehearsals get a bit too exciting for me."

"Why is that?" Alice's eyes grew round.

"My last rehearsal," Louise said, "was a complete debacle."

"It wasn't really that bad." Jane cast Louise a sympathetic look. "After all, you only needed two days to calm down afterward," she teased.

Alice laughed, and Louise cast Jane a stony glare. "It was not funny."

"Oh, all right. It was not funny and I'm a horrible person for laughing. But"—Jane held up a plate of steaming chocolate-chip waffles—"I'm a horrible person who can cook!"

When Alice called the vet's office, the receptionist told her to bring Miracle in that very morning at eleven. They would make time to see her.

So at eleven, Alice loaded the dog and kennel into her blue Toyota and set off to see the veterinarian. As she drove, she reflected on how odd it was to be driving around Acorn Hill again. It also felt quite strange to be driving such a small, maneuverable vehicle after spending so many hours taking turns with June driving the SUV. If she were still at camp, she would be finishing working in the CCU and probably would be out under the canopy helping to wash mountains of bowls. She wondered how many of her friends were still there.

As she pulled into a parking space, she remembered that she wanted to e-mail Ellen and the twins today. She'd have to get Jane to oversee the process and make sure she didn't foul up anything. The electronic age and Alice were not on easy terms yet, but she was determined to overcome her hesitations.

She opened the door of Miracle's kennel and attached a real leash to the new collar the little dog wore. Jane had run out to a store late the day before and returned home with both items. "Let's go, little miss," she said.

Miracle trotted across the lot and entered the clinic with Alice, staying close to her left side as if she'd had dozens of obedience lessons. Perhaps she had. A large dog leaped to its feet and began barking wildly the moment it spied Miracle, but the cocker spaniel merely shot it a contemptuous glance and walked right by.

Alice had to laugh. "You really do think you're a queen," she murmured. "Don't you?"

Miracle looked up at her as if to say, "Well, of course."

The receptionist gave Alice a clipboard and pen with an information sheet attached. Most of the information included things Alice could not answer, like the dog's age and when or whether she had been vaccinated. Alice hoped there was nothing wrong with her other than the tumor, but who knew?

She led Miracle to a seat. The moment Alice sat, the little dog leaped into her lap, sitting there as if she had been doing it for years. Alice noticed the position allowed her to look down on the larger dog, who continued to bark sporadically. Fortunately, the other dog soon was called into the examining room. After a short wait, an assistant showed Alice into a second exam room. The young woman weighed Miracle by having her step onto a large metal rectangle near the floor. When the tech was done, she put her foot on a lever and the metal tray rose slowly with a quiet whirring sound until it became an exam table at waist height.

The assistant left the room. Just as Alice began to wonder how long the exam might be, a pleasant-looking woman in her fifties strode in. "Good morning. I'm Dr. Spence."

Alice shook her hand. "Alice Howard. And this is Miracle."

"Hello, Miracle," the vet said. She glanced over the information Alice had provided. "So this little lady is a hurricane survivor." She shook her head. "I imagine you had quite an experience down at that rescue center."

Alice nodded. "It was…busy." She was struck once again by the inadequacy of language. How could she possibly convey a real sense of the experience?

"I bet it was. Did you see a lot of injuries?"

Alice shook her head. "Some, but most of the animals were starving or dehydrated. As many as half of them couldn't walk when they arrived."

Dr. Spence's eyes widened. "Were there a lot you couldn't save?"

"Oh no." Alice was glad to be able to be positive. "In the two weeks I was there, we only lost one dog. We had a couple of animals that were touch-and-go for a few days though."

"That's quite an accomplishment," the doctor said. "I thank the Lord for people like you." She looked down at Miracle. "So tell me about this little lady. She has a tumor, you say?"

Alice nodded. "We know very little about her. She was found loose in a backyard, so we don't know whether that was her home or just a place she ended up after the storm. I think she was an indoor pet. She is housebroken and seems comfortable indoors." As the vet reached for Miracle, Alice said, "And she's not always great with strangers."

"Okay. Why don't I get someone in here to hold her so I can do a thorough exam?"

Alice nodded. She had seen Gina restrain dogs, but she didn't have the experience, and the last thing she wanted was for the vet to get bitten. In short order, the young assistant returned. She efficiently held Miracle immobile while the vet checked her eyes, ears and teeth, and gave the tumor on her belly a thorough study. She ran her hands over all of the dog's limbs, then straightened and said to Alice, "I need to take a sample of that tumor so we can biopsy it, but it needs to come off no matter the prognosis. I would like to schedule a surgery as soon as possible to remove the whole thing. I also would like to do blood work, because she appears to be an older animal. I want to check for heartworm."

"She was wormed at the camp but not tested for heartworms," Alice said. "And she didn't receive any vaccines." She hesitated. "The vets at the camp thought the tumor might be malignant."

The vet heard her unspoken question. "We'll know better once we biopsy it, but I'll be honest with you, it doesn't look good to me." The doctor opened the door to the back where Alice caught a glimpse of stainless steel, blue scrubs and several people scurrying around. "This only will take a few minutes."

The technician set Miracle on the floor. The little dog looked back at Alice as if to say, "How could you do this to me?" but walked away with the young woman in a surprisingly docile manner.

Chapter Sixteen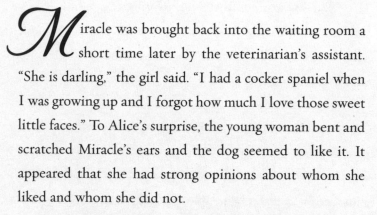

Miracle was brought back into the waiting room a short time later by the veterinarian's assistant. "She is darling," the girl said. "I had a cocker spaniel when I was growing up and I forgot how much I love those sweet little faces." To Alice's surprise, the young woman bent and scratched Miracle's ears and the dog seemed to like it. It appeared that she had strong opinions about whom she liked and whom she did not.

A moment later, the vet also approached.

"I'll let you know as soon as possible on the heartworm test." The woman held out her hand. "I think it was a wonderful thing you did."

"Thank you so much." Alice was touched by the vet's words.

"I don't think we should wait to remove that tumor. Even if it is benign, it is growing and I'd like to get it off. I have surgeries on Friday. Could we schedule her then?"

"I don't see why not." Alice looked down at Miracle. "The sooner we can get her healthy, the better. Then it would be best to settle her in a foster home before she gets too attached to my sisters and me."

"Do you have any prospects?"

"Not yet," Alice admitted.

"Why don't you put a poster on our bulletin board? Have any interested folks talk to the girls at the desk. That way, we can prescreen potential homes for you. There are some homes that we know wouldn't be suitable and others we wouldn't hesitate to recommend."

"That would be wonderful," Alice said.

"She's already had enough traumas in her little life," the vet said. She bent to stroke Miracle's head but hastily withdrew her hand when Miracle curled her lip and uttered a low, warning growl. The vet laughed. "After what this old girl has been through, I suppose she is entitled to be a bit cranky with me."

"I appreciate all your help," Alice said. "We want to find the very best home for her that we possibly can."

∽

"Wish me luck." Louise looked as if she were readying for a confrontation rather than going to a rehearsal after dinner.

"Luck," Jane said. "Don't worry, Louie. I have a feeling it's going to go better this evening."

"I surely hope so. Karin is over her illness, so there will be two of us again. That alone gives me comfort." She paused. "Would it be really, really wrong of me to wish the Trimble brothers would catch whatever she had?"

Alice and Jane burst out laughing.

"Beyond wrong," Alice said. "Now go on. Jane and I will say a prayer for you."

"I'm going to need it," Louise muttered beneath her breath as she selected her gray wool dress coat from the closet.

But her sisters' prayers must have worked. As the children filed into the Assembly Room a short time later, they all seemed happy and ready to rehearse. Even Morley Trimble was cheerful.

"I got three dollars from my daddy for being brave at the doctor!" he told Louise.

Her eyebrows rose. "Indeed."

Karin Lindars chuckled. "Inflation, just like the tooth fairy. When I was small, I got Swedish currency worth about two cents American. Now the kids get dollars."

The last child arrived.

"All right, boys and girls." Louise clapped her hands. "Tonight I would like to rehearse all the group songs quickly, and then practice our processional. Afterward, everyone but the soloists may be dismissed."

They practiced "The night goes with weighty step" and the lovely round she had found, "Santa Lucia, thy light is glowing." She was surprised, pleasantly so, at how well most of the children knew the lyrics. She had given each family a printout with the songs on it, but she really had not expected that the children would practice diligently. Apparently, she had underestimated them.

"Very nice job!" she told her young charges. "Now let's line up and we'll sing 'Hark! Through the Darksome Night' as we process. Do you all remember your places in the line?"

They did. Louise barely could conceal her relief.

Karin, who skillfully lined up the children, was smiling. "This is going to be lovely."

"How are the costumes coming along?"

"Quite well. We are using a set of old children's choir robes for all of them. A friend of mine has borrowed them from a church in Lancaster. Mrs. Trimble is making long wands for all the star boys. I admit it gives me pause thinking of handing long sticks to all those active little guys."

Louise laughed. "Yes, I can understand that."

"I bought tinsel for all the girls except the Lucia, and we're using a wide red ribbon for her sash. The only part that is giving me problems is the Lucia's crown."

"How so?"

"I've tried using a number of things to fashion a circlet that would hold those battery-operated candles, but I can't seem to get it right."

"What did you use in Minnesota?"

"Each year, one family loaned us a crown that had been passed down through the generations but I have had no luck locating anyone here who has something like that."

Louise thought for a moment. "What about using the frame of an Advent wreath? It is open in the center for the Christ candle, so it probably would fit down over Marit's head far enough and there are four candleholders on it. Perhaps we could use craft glue to affix the electric candles to it. Once it is covered with greens, no one will be able to see the frame anyway."

"That's a wonderful idea. I wonder where I could get an Advent wreath frame."

"Why don't we check with Rev. Thompson? Perhaps there is something suitable here at the chapel."

After several practices of the processional, Louise dismissed the children, keeping Marit and two other girls for a bit of one-on-one work. Finally, she was satisfied with the songs. The other soloists left, and Marit settled down with a book to wait for her mother.

Karin and Louise settled onto chairs in the front row to review their plans. Costumes and the service were in good shape.

"I gave your recipe to Jane," Louise told Karin. "She will bake the saffron buns."

"And I am making gingerbread. I'll do a punch too."

"Decorations. Are there any traditional ones?" Louise asked. "In my research, I found very little about decor. Apples and eucalyptus were mentioned, I believe."

"Since the Lucia's sash is red, we could make eucalyptus swags to hang on the pews and decorate them with red ribbons. In addition, I saw some lovely miniature apples at a store in Riverton the other day. Those would brighten the swags a bit."

"That sounds lovely." Louise was delighted. "There is just one small problem."

Karin looked puzzled. "What's that?"

"We are not going to be able to find anyone to help make them until after the crafts fair, I suspect. My sister Jane seems to have asked every person in the congregation to make something for the event."

Karin laughed. "Yes. I'm making hand-dipped candles for it."

"See?"

"Leave it to me, Louise. I will line up a few mothers to help put them together the week after the craft show. I can't thank you enough for your help. This is going to be beautiful."

"Yes, it will. And it has been fun, hasn't it? Well, parts of it have been fun," Louise said, smiling. "I think it will be a lovely addition to Grace Chapel's holiday traditions."

༄

The excited babble of adolescent girls' voices greeted Alice the moment she walked into the ANGELs' meeting at seven o'clock Wednesday evening.

"Miss Howard!"

"We missed you!"

"You're back!"

Alice smiled. "I missed all of you too."

"What was it like?"

"Did you bring back any pets?"

"Was it scary?"

"Did you see hurt animals?"

Alice supposed she had not realized how many people in the community were interested in and aware of the trip she and June had made. She gathered the girls around her and gave them a short talk about her adventure and all the things that had been involved.

Britt Nilsen, Ingrid's mother, who had helped with the girls' bracelet project in Alice's absence, appeared fascinated too.

"How long are they going to need people in Florida?" she asked Alice after the girls had gone to their seats.

Alice sensed more than causal interest behind the question. "Volunteers are going to be needed for weeks yet, if not months," she told Britt. "They still are finding animals alive, and all the rescue sites like Camp Compassion are chock-full of rescued animals with no homes. Rescue groups are taking some, but if owners don't show up, they all will have to be cared for until they can be adopted into new homes."

"I would like to talk more about it with you when you have time." Britt smiled. "You have inspired me, Alice. There is no reason I could not go down there and help for a week. My children aren't babies anymore."

Alice was thrilled. "Oh, Britt, that would be wonderful. Why don't you come over to the inn anytime tomorrow morning? I have to work at two, but until then I'll just be working around the inn and I would be happy to tell you about it in detail."

Britt smiled. "Thank you, Alice. It's a date. Now I'll make myself scarce and let the girls show you what they have made for the crafts fair."

Alice bid her good-bye and moved to the table Britt had indicated.

Ingrid, Britt's daughter, took her hand. "We worked hard on these. I did that one and that one there." She pointed to two of the many macramé bracelets on display.

"Girls! You really are angels," Alice said. "I had no idea you would be able to make so many of these in such a short time."

On the table before her were more than two dozen of the pretty bracelets braided and knotted with embroidery floss in all colors of the rainbow. One in shades of aqua and blue caught her eye. The colors should not have gone well together but they looked fabulous. There were equally lovely pinks, browns, brilliant greens and yellows, magentas, purples and many, many more. Alice picked up one after another, marveling at the color pairings and the intricacy of the knots.

"My sister, Ms. Howard, will be thrilled with these," she finally said. "She is the person in charge of gathering crafts to sell. Oh, I do have one request from her. Vendors are being asked to donate one of their items for a raffle. Why don't we choose a bracelet for the raffle and then talk about a price for the rest? My sister may have a different price in mind, but I am certain she will be willing to consider your recommendations. While we're chatting, we can pin them to this piece of foam board. They'll be easy to see against the white background."

❧

At home that evening, Alice took the bracelet display to the kitchen for Jane to see. Louise was giving a piano lesson with the parlor door open, and Alice could hear a student dutifully hammering out a tune.

"They are beautiful!" Jane ran a gentle finger over them. "And see how professional the handiwork looks. No one will believe twelve- and thirteen-year-old girls made these. These will sell in a heartbeat, Alice."

"Oh, good. I'll tell the girls." Alice pulled out one that had a small tag dangling from it. "They would like to give this one to the raffle."

"Wow! This is pretty," Jane said, noting the soft shades of pink and lavender in the design. "Just between you and me, I think the raffle could end up being our biggest moneymaker. We have received some beautiful things."

"You're doing such a good job with this, Jane. Aunt Ethel was wise to choose you to head up the committee."

"Honestly," said Jane, "I couldn't have done it without Sylvia and Florence. Sylvia volunteered, of course, but Florence has been such a surprise. She really has pulled out all the stops to find crafters, both to display and to donate."

"She isn't about to let Aunt Ethel get all the credit for the success of this show," Alice said, chuckling. "For once their competitive natures are complementing each other."

There was a reflective silence in the kitchen, broken by a sigh from Jane. "I do wish Aunt Ethel could see how much she has hurt Louise. I believe she really thinks Louise owes her an apology."

"But I thought Louise said she did apologize that day." Alice's tone was a bit less mild than normal.

"She did, but Aunt Ethel doesn't recall that. All she remembers is that Louise walked away and would not talk to her. She seems to have conveniently forgotten the hurtful things she said. I know Louise has tried to forgive her, but matters still aren't right between them."

Alice sighed. "Oh for heaven's sake. I'm tempted to put them together in a small room and not let them come out until they are friends again."

"The idea has merit." Jane grinned. "But only if I get to watch. And listen." Then she set aside the bracelet board and covered one of Alice's hands with her own. "How are you doing? You seem…I don't know…so sad a lot of the time."

"I'm not sad…it's just that…" Alice turned her hand over and clasped Jane's hand in return, grateful for the small act of comfort. "It's hard to leap back into one's life without a care in the world after seeing such suffering. Despite all the hardships, I wonder if I need to be back down there."

"Have you talked to June?"

Alice shook her head. "She went to visit her son and daughter since she missed Thanksgiving. I think she's due back this weekend."

"Maybe you could get together. Or maybe"—Jane's face lit up—"you should call Shelby, the woman you talked to before you went. I bet she could relate to how you feel."

Alice regarded her sister in surprise. "That's a terrific idea. I don't know why I didn't think of that. I would love to see her."

"She called here once while you were gone. She laughed when I told her you were staying another week. She said she would still be there if she could be."

Alice rose quickly and picked up the phone. "I'm going to call her right now." Then she stopped, a rather sheepish expression crossing her face. "Except that I don't know what I did with her telephone number."

"The phone book is beneath the desk," Jane said helpfully, though she knew full well Alice could find it.

It was silly to be so excited, Alice thought as she looked up Riverly in the telephone book and punched the buttons of Shelby's number.

$\backsim$

The veterinarian's receptionist called Thursday afternoon to remind Alice not to feed the cocker any breakfast Friday.

Miracle was less than happy when Alice did not appear to notice her hunger pangs the next morning. The little dog followed Alice from room to room, looking woebegone.

During breakfast, Miracle sat hopefully by Alice's chair for a while. Finally, realizing she was getting nowhere, the cocker spaniel went over to the rug in front of the back door and flopped down with a huge groan.

"What on earth is wrong with that poor dog?" Louise asked.

"She goes in for surgery today," Alice said, "and she is not allowed to have anything to eat this morning. I feel like a criminal."

"You'd feel even worse if she faced a nastier fate," Louise said.

Alice bobbed her head in acknowledgment. "Trust you to put it in perspective."

"Have you made any progress in looking for a home for her?" Louise looked over at the little dog with an expression that actually appeared to reveal fondness.

"Not that we're anxious to get rid of her," Jane said. "She's really been very pleasant. At times I forget she's here."

"I made a flyer concerning her," Alice said. "Jane, could you help me produce it on the computer so it looks nice?"

"Sure," Jane said. "We can use Publisher."

"Of course, I'll want to wait until after this surgery to see what her prognosis is."

"If it's...poor," Louise said, "what will you do?"

Alice felt a lump rise in her throat. "I'm not sure," she said. "Any foster home would have to be very special to take her in knowing they might have her only a short time."

There was a glum silence around the table.

Then Jane said, "If that's the case, would you have to give her away?"

"It wouldn't seem right," Louise said. "If she is not going to live long, Alice, you should keep her here with you, where she is already comfortable and settled in."

Alice was stunned. "You wouldn't mind that?"

"Of course not," Louise and Jane said in unison.

"I don't know what to say. I promised you I wouldn't bring any animals home, and I broke my promise. I appreciate your forbearance."

Jane grinned. "And do you think we believed for one minute that old softhearted Alice would come home from caring for a bunch of rescued animals empty-handed?"

Louise laughed.

Alice felt sheepish. "You know me too well, I suppose." She glanced back over at the dog. "I did get one bit of good news when the vet called. They took blood and did several tests on her. Everything looked normal for an older animal and she tested negative for heartworm, which is a particularly nasty parasite."

"How old does the vet think she is?"

"She couldn't tell me exactly, but she thinks Miracle is between seven and nine or so."

"So in dog years," Jane said, "she's about our age."

Louise's eyebrows rose. "Indeed. That's fitting."

❧

Alice spent an anxious day wondering how Miracle's surgery had gone. In late afternoon, the inn's telephone rang. Jane started to say, "I'll get it," but Alice was rushing across the room already.

"Hello?"

"Alice, this is Sallie at Dr. Spence's office. We won't have the results of the biopsy for a few days, but I wanted to let you know Miracle did just fine with her surgery."

"Oh, that's wonderful news. When can I take her home?"

"Why don't you wait until close to six before you pick her up?" the assistant suggested. "She's still pretty groggy from the anesthesia, and we're going to want to get some pain meds into her before she leaves."

"Will I need to give her more at home?"

"Probably for the first day or so, but you'll be able to sneak them into her food, I suspect. Is she a good eater?"

Alice laughed. "My sister Jane says her nickname should be Hoover. She inhales her food."

The girl laughed. "Good. She probably won't even notice there's a pill in there!"

❧

The next day, Louise and Alice both helped Jane serve breakfast, because they had a full house over the weekend. But shortly before nine, she said, "I have to excuse myself now and get over to the chapel. Today is the final dress rehearsal for the Lucia pageant."

"Are you ready?" Jane looked up from the fruit salad on which she was putting the final touches.

"I think so." Louise smiled. "No one threw up at the last rehearsal, so we got a lot done. Today is just a matter of putting it all together."

"I can't wait to see it. I'm planning to make the *Lussekatters* this afternoon. I think it's a wonderful idea to share a different cultural experience with our congregation."

"I agree. I am so glad Karin Lindars suggested it. I have enjoyed getting to know her too. Marit, the daughter who is going to be the Lucia, plays piano. Karin asked me if I would consider taking her on as a student."

"Do you have a space in your schedule?"

"Yes, I can fit her in." Louise rose. "I will see you after the rehearsal. If you need any help with the saffron buns, I shall be available this afternoon."

"Thanks," Jane said. "The recipe looks simple and won't take very long at all, but I might enlist you to help me decorate boxes for the raffle tickets if you wouldn't mind."

"I'd be happy to help."

"So would I," Alice said as she came through the swinging door that led from the kitchen into the dining room. She was carrying stacks of dirty plates in both hands. "Breakfast was a success," she told her sisters. "Jane, they loved the egg casserole."

"I did too," Louise said. "Where did you find that recipe, Jane?"

"In a Lancaster paper. I altered it a little bit, though."

"And I bet it is better now than the original," Louise said knowingly.

Chapter Seventeen

S aturday's rehearsal was in the sanctuary, where the service would take place the following afternoon. All the children were excited as they donned their white robes before rehearsal. Some of the girls twirled about, setting the robes flying.

"Oh dear," said Karin, pointing at Abby Waller. "That robe is going to have to be altered. It's one of the two small-est ones we had and it's still too long." Abby was in first grade, but she was the smallest girl in the group.

Karin bustled over to the child and spoke for a moment, then lifted the little girl onto the closest pew and knelt before her. Karin had arrived with long chains of safety pins attached to the front of her sweatshirt. Louise was not sure about the fashion statement that made, but now she saw how practical it was. Karin efficiently turned up the hem of the robe, pinning it in place in just a few minutes so Abby would not trip over it.

One of the Trimbles and the youngest Dawson were using their star wands for swordplay, which Louise stopped with a firm admonishment. Then she gathered the children around. "It's time to line up. Does everyone remember whom they stand behind?"

Children scurried back and forth as they dashed to find their places in line. When the bustle abated, one child stood off to one side, looking bewildered.

"Who remembers where Bill belongs?" Louise called.

"Up there," said Delissa. "He's the line leader."

However, the little boy hung back, his thumb in his mouth, when Louise placed a hand on his shoulder and urged him into position. "Doan wanna be the line leader," he said.

"Well, that's a first," Karin commented. "Usually they fight over the chance to lead the class."

Louise knelt before the child. "You get to be the first one to walk in," she told him. "It's an important job and I need someone I can count on to be first."

But Bill shook his head. "Doan wanna."

"He's afraid of all the people that are going to be here," said his cousin.

"Oh." Louise knew a moment of doubt. This did not bode well.

"Could he trade places with Abby?" Karin was eyeing the children.

Louise eyed the two children. She had lined them up carefully by ascending height...but did it really matter if the first child was a hair taller than the second one? "That is an excellent idea," she told Karin. "Abby, would you like to lead the procession?" she asked the little girl.

Abby bounced on her toes. Her hair, tied up in two high ponytails, swung wildly. "Yeth!" she said, grinning and displaying two missing front teeth.

"All right." Louise guided Bill into the line behind Abby. "This will be better," she told him. "You just follow her, all right?"

He nodded solemnly, the thumb still tucked firmly into his mouth.

"Boys and girls," Louise said. "When the program begins, I will be up front at the piano. Mrs. Lindars will tell you when to start. Try to keep an arm's length between you and the boy or girl in front of you." Immediately, all the children began to hold an arm up, measuring an arm's length. "Don't forget to sing as you walk. Who remembers the first song?"

A child's hand shot into the air. For the next few minutes, Louise reviewed the words to the songs. When she was satisfied, she went to the piano at the front of the room. "Quiet," she called. "I'm going to start."

The rehearsal went well, in Louise's opinion. She considered herself a strict taskmaster, but still she thought the children had done nicely. They were ready for tomorrow.

⌒

Later that afternoon, Alice drove to June's house.

June had returned from her son's home the previous evening and was enthusiastic when Alice suggested getting together with Shelby. "Oh, it's good to see you," June cried as Alice got out of her car. She rushed down her front walk, her short blonde hair flying around her head, and embraced Alice. "Just look at you! All dressed up with your hair washed and a little touch of lip gloss and *real shoes*."

Alice was laughing. "I never thought I'd see the day when tan slacks and a heavy navy sweater were dressy."

June indicated the simple skirt and blouse she was wearing beneath her quilted jacket. "I realized this is the first time in almost three weeks I have worn a skirt. It doesn't feel right," she confessed.

"I've missed you," Alice said. "I've missed camp. I've missed all our friends."

"Me too," June said. "I'm afraid I bored my children silly talking about Camp Compassion."

"My sisters have been good listeners," Alice told her friend, "but I don't want to challenge their patience."

"Hello, you two!" Shelby Riverly climbed out of a small sedan she had parked behind Alice's car.

"Hello," June and Alice called together.

"Come on in," June said, and the three women went up the pretty brick walk and into June's little house. It was not exactly a cottage, but that was what came to Alice's mind. June had a green thumb, and all spring and summer the

house was surrounded by beautiful swaths of colorful flow-
ers. Even now, in early December, she still had some
chrysanthemums and ornamental cabbage lending color to
the brown landscape. At one side of the yard stood a lovely
juniper. On the other a cypress swayed in a gentle breeze.

A wreath of pretty boughs graced her dark-green front
door. It bore clusters of dark-red berries and a huge red bow.

June already had done her Christmas decorating inside
as well. She had put up an artificial tree and decorated it in
a Victorian motif, with dusty pink, shiny glass spheres and
tiny ivory crocheted ornaments. Alice made a mental note
to mention the Victorian tree to her sisters. Beneath it, an
HO-scale train ran in a circle through a little village. The
whole set was nestled on fluffy white cotton that gave the
appearance of snow.

When Alice complimented her on her energy in having
decorated already, June thanked her, then laughed. "Those
trains are not for my entertainment. My grandson is crazy
about railroads. He says he wants to be an engineer when
he grows up. This set belonged to my grandfather, and
someday I'll pass it on to Paulie. Please," she added, "have a
seat. I made us some hot chocolate and Christmas cookies.
They're low-calorie," she added solemnly, and both Alice
and Shelby chuckled.

After the initial flurry of small talk and passing around
refreshments, Shelby said, "I have something for you two."

She bent and began digging around in the enormous shoulder bag that Alice recalled from the first time they met. "Joe e-mailed me. He said you mentioned that you rarely use e-mail, and he wanted you to have these. I told him I'd print them out for you." She handed Alice an envelope that felt too thick and heavy to be a sheet or two of paper, then handed a similar package to June.

Alice opened the flap and drew out the contents. "Oh," she said. "Oh, Shelby, how thoughtful. Thank you so much."

"This is going to make me cry." June was as moved as Alice was.

Joe had sent pictures, which Shelby printed. Alice slowly examined them, touched by the gesture. "Look, June! Here we are trying to put up our tent. Thank heavens Mark was there to help us. And this one was taken at intake one night. Let's see, it's the little Yorkie, so it must have been my first night there."

"Here we are at Bible study," June added, "and we certainly look a little worse for the wear!"

"I have one of those too," Alice said. "And look at this." She shook her head as she pointed to the picture, even though she knew Shelby must have seen them already. "I had no idea someone was taking pictures. This was the day Riley fell off the roof."

"What? That picture is of Riley? Was he hurt?"

The photo showed Alice kneeling on the ground and bending over someone whose face was obscured by the bush that several of the men were cutting away. She was wrapping his arm, which she recalled doing to stabilize him for transport. "He broke his arm," Alice told her. "He fell into this bush—which is no longer there—and he was really lucky because it broke his fall. He could have been hurt much worse." She looked at Shelby and smiled. "By the time we left, he was rushing around like he always does."

"You know," Shelby said, "it's so odd to see people I know in these photos interspersed with so many people I don't know. It is hard to believe how many volunteers keep arriving."

"It was quite a revolving door," June agreed.

"I found it so inspiring," Alice told them. "How often do you see God's work in the world in such a concrete way? I hope the camp continues to get more volunteers. I spoke with a woman who seemed as if she might commit to making a trip." She smiled, reaching over and squeezing Shelby's hand. "I'm spreading the word, just as you did for me."

"That's good," Shelby said. "I wish I could go back. But I can't leave my children again. My mother-in-law is a saint, but her health isn't that great, and I can't ask her to watch two small children for a week or more."

"I'm struggling with that feeling too," Alice told her friends. "Part of me recognizes that I'm needed here, both at the hospital and at the inn. However, another part of me feels compelled to go back. It's almost as if I don't quite fit here anymore."

June smiled sadly. "Exactly. An experience like the one we had alters you forever. The only other people who can understand are others who shared it."

Shelby nodded, her eyes sympathetic.

It was an enormous relief to Alice to hear someone else voice the feelings with which she had been struggling. "Will it get better?" she asked Shelby. "Will I stop feeling tearful and heartbroken soon? I just can't seem to stop thinking of it."

"I can't answer that. Each of us deals with the feelings in a unique way. I have seen this among the friends I've stayed in touch with. But I believe that if you follow the pattern most people do, the compulsion to return will fade in a few weeks. It just takes time to find the 'old you' again."

"Thank you, Shelby," Alice said. "I've needed that reassurance."

"We absolutely need to get more comfortable using e-mail," June said to Alice. "Ellen and several other people gave me their e-mail addresses. I don't know about you, but it would make me feel better to be in contact with them."

Alice nodded. "I suppose I can manage e-mail. I don't want to lose touch with Ellen, and I know younger people today don't write letters anymore."

"Way to be proactive." Shelby smiled. "So tell me all about your trip now. I want to hear every little detail."

∽

The following morning, the sisters walked home for Sunday dinner after the morning service drew to a close. All of their guests had checked out, and no more would arrive until Tuesday.

By suppertime, it was obvious that Louise was somewhat uneasy about that evening's performance. Jane cooked roast beef accompanied by twice-baked potatoes sprinkled with chopped chives for supper, but Louise barely could eat a bite.

"It's not like you to be nervous before a performance," Alice said as they put on their coats before heading over to the chapel shortly before seven.

"It's not my own performing I worry about!" Louise said with a half laugh. "It's those two dozen unpredictable little people."

Jane patted her sister's shoulder. "I'm sure it's going to go just fine. You said the dress rehearsal yesterday morning went well."

"It did," said Louise, "but I have learned that one never knows."

When they arrived at the chapel, Alice and Jane went to sit in their usual pew, while Louise headed straight for the Assembly Room, which was serving as the dressing room for the Santa Lucia ceremony.

As seven o'clock approached, the chapel filled with many of the same people who regularly attended on Sunday mornings, plus a few additional family members and friends of the participants.

The lights dimmed.

Then, from the back of the church, the faraway sound of high, sweet voices singing was heard. Alice realized the children had begun singing as they left the Assembly Room for the front door of the church. The sound swelled as they drew closer, and the words became clear:

> Hark! Through the darksome night
> Sounds come a winging:
> Lo! 'tis the Queen of Light
> Joyfully singing.
> Clad in her garment white,
> Wearing her crown of light,
> Santa Lucia, Santa Lucia!

> Deep in the northern sky
> Bright stars are beaming;
> Christmas is drawing nigh
> Candles are gleaming.
> Welcome thou vision rare,
> Lights glowing in thy hair.
> Santa Lucia, Santa Lucia!

Light pierced the darkness of the chapel. One by one, a stately line of white-robed children processed up the aisle, sweetly singing the words of the song. They all wore crowns of tinsel, and the girls wore tinsel sashes with long, shining tails. The girls held small arrangements of greenery, each with a battery-powered candle rising from its center. The boys carried long wands with glittering, iridescent stars at the tips. The stars caught the brightness from the candles and reflected it in myriad points of light.

The children formed a choir on the steps of the altar, the smallest first with a gradually taller group moving in and filling the space behind them. Finally, a tall, slender young girl wearing a red sash over her white robe came up the aisle of the darkened church. On her head was a crown of greens with four glowing candles that made the girl's face and hair radiant. She carried a basket lined with a white cloth and filled with shiny red apples and some of the sweet-smelling saffron buns Jane had made.

As the children finished their song, the girl with the red sash stepped forward. "I represent Santa Lucia, or Saint Lucy," she said. "Welcome to the first Grace Chapel Santa Lucia service."

Another girl, one of Alice's ANGELs, moved to the lectern, where she read a traditional story about the origins of the legend of Santa Lucia. She then explained the customs of the people of Sweden.

Next, two older girls came forward. Both of them were among Alice's ANGELs. The first sang the opening verse of a song a cappella in a pure, clear soprano:

> The night goes with weighty step
> round yard and hearth,
> round earth, the sun departs
> and leaves the woods brooding.
> There in our dark house,
> appears with lighted candles
> Saint Lucia, Saint Lucia.

Then she faded back and the second girl stepped forward to sing another verse:

> The night goes great and mute
> now hear it swings

> in every silent room
> murmurs as if from wings.
> Look! At our threshold stands
> white-clad with lights in her hair
> Saint Lucia, Saint Lucia.

At the conclusion of the second verse, the other girl came forward again. In unison, the two girls sang a third and final verse together:

> The darkness shall soon depart
> from the earth's valleys
> thus she speaks
> a wonderful word to us.
> The day shall rise anew
> from the rosy sky.
> Saint Lucia, Saint Lucia.

Next, three children approached the lectern. Stepping onto a stool that allowed him to be seen over the top, the first boy said, "The theme of light is very important to our Christian faith. Hear the Word of God in the following passages from the Bible."

The second child stepped up. She turned to a new page in the Bible and read from Genesis 1:3: "'And God said, "Let there be light," and there was light.'"

And finally, another child ascended to the lectern.

"Psalm 18:24–25, 28, 30: 'The LORD has rewarded me according to my righteousness, according to the cleanness of my hands in his sight. To the faithful, you show yourself faithful…You, O LORD, keep my lamp burning; my God turns my darkness into light…As for God, his way is perfect; the word of the LORD is flawless. He is a shield for all who take refuge in him.'"

As the little boy stepped back into his place in the group, Louise began to play the piano. The children separated into two groups, one on the left, one on the right. On Louise's signal, they all sang together:

Santa Lucia, thy light is glowing
Through darkest winter night, comfort bestowing.
Dreams float on dreams tonight,
Comes then the morning light,
Santa Lucia, Santa Lucia.

As they began to sing it through a second time, only the group of children on the right side sang. Halfway through, the second group of children began, and Alice realized the selection was a round that created a beautiful harmony. At the conclusion of the round, the children's voices merged again into one melody. Marit Lindars, the Lucia, walked to the lectern and read what was arguably the best-known passage about light from the book of Matthew:

"'You are the light of the world. A city on a hill cannot be hidden. Neither do people light a lamp and put it under a bowl. Instead they put it on its stand, and it gives light to everyone in the house. In the same way, let your light shine before men, that they may see your good deeds and praise your Father in heaven'" (Matthew 5:14–16).

Then she stepped to the center of the altar again. Taking one of the saffron rolls from her basket, she held it aloft. "You are invited to the Assembly Room at the conclusion of this ceremony to partake of several traditional foods associated with the Santa Lucia celebration in Sweden."

She replaced the roll in her basket. Once again, Louise played an introduction on the piano. The children began to sing one final time:

> The night treads heavily
> around yards and dwellings
> In places unreached by sun,
> the shadows brood
> Into our dark house she comes,
> bearing lighted candles,
> Saint Lucia, Saint Lucia.

They slowly filed out, taking all light with them and leaving the chapel in darkness for one long, humming moment before Karin, at the back of the church, turned up the lights and the congregation began to buzz enthusiastically about the remarkable experience they had just enjoyed.

Chapter Eighteen

*L*ouise! That was fabulous!" Jane and Alice converged on their elder sister enthusiastically in the Assembly Room at the conclusion of the Santa Lucia service.

Louise was flushed and smiling. "Tell Karin that," she said modestly. "She was the one who came up with the idea."

"It really was marvelous," Alice said. "Where did you find all that music?"

"Most of it came from that book I found at the Potterston library. And the rest came from the online sources Jane helped me locate."

Louise suddenly fell silent, her face losing its happy glow.

Puzzled, Alice glanced around—and saw their aunt across the room. Alice looked at Louise's downcast face and then over at Ethel's furrowed brow.

"You know," she said to Jane in an undertone, "I realize that I am known as a peaceful person, but I am just about ready to knock two heads together."

"May I help?" Jane asked facetiously.

Alice began to stride across the room, but before she could take more than a few steps, Ethel came walking toward the three sisters. She held out a hand to Louise.

"You did a fine job putting the Santa Lucia service together, Louise. What a delightful addition to the Christmas season."

Louise looked surprised. More than surprised, Alice thought, astonished. She clasped Ethel's hand and allowed the older woman to pull her into a hug. "Thank you, Aunt Ethel."

"Louise…" Ethel hesitated. "I mistook your desire to help me with the craft show for interference. I guess I was just so determined to do it my way that I wasn't willing to accept suggestions, no matter how well intended. I apologize for hurting your feelings with angry words."

"Oh, Aunt Ethel," Louise said, "don't apologize. I know my suggestions can sound awfully heavy-handed. My only excuse is that it seemed like such a big project, and I was so worried it would be too much to put together in such a short time. But from what I can see, you have done a fine job of organizing it. I, too, am sorry for our misunderstanding."

Ethel's face softened as she looked at her three nieces. "I know I drive you crazy sometimes," she said with a smile, "but wouldn't life be boring without me?"

The Tuesday following the Lucia service, Alice worked a day shift. As she was letting herself into the house in midafternoon, the telephone rang.

"Grace Chapel Inn, Alice speaking. May I help you?"

"Alice Howard?"

"Yes."

"Just the person I had hoped to find! This is Dr. Spence."

"Hello, Dr.— Oh! Do you have news for me?"

"I do." The vet's voice was sober. "The tumor is malignant, as we suspected. However, it does not appear to have spread. I biopsied the areas around the edges of the excision, and I believe we have gotten all the diseased tissue. Only time will tell, but your little dog should have a number of good senior years ahead of her."

Alice let out a sigh. "Oh, thank you, Dr. Spence, thank you so much! Is she in any pain?"

"No, she's resting comfortably. By the way, I have someone else here who would like to speak to you."

Mystified, Alice waited while the vet transferred the telephone.

"Hello? Miss Howard? This is Sallie. I don't know if you remember me, but I am the technician who helped with Miracle the other day."

"Of course, Sallie." Alice did indeed recall the dark-haired young woman. "Miracle liked you."

Sallie laughed. "I guess that might make me memorable since you say she's not fond of many people. Miss Howard, I wondered if…well, I would like to offer Miracle a foster home until her family can find her. And if they never do appear, I would be interested in adopting her."

Alice was stunned. She had been praying for such an event, and this exceeded her greatest hopes. Sallie had medical knowledge and a close relationship with the dog's vet. "Oh, Sallie, this is wonderful news. I can't think of any-one I'd rather have care for Miracle."

"I'm glad you feel that way, Miss Howard. Is there a foster care form to fill out?"

"Yes," Alice told her. "I do have an application for you. When it's complete, I'll send it down to Florida to the director of Camp Compassion, and once he approves it, Miracle can go to live with you."

"Wonderful! May I visit her in the meantime? I thought it might be best if I saw her in her own familiar surroundings initially. Then you could bring her to visit me a few times before she comes here for good. That would be the least stressful way to introduce her to a new home, don't you think?"

"I certainly do." Alice's pulse was pounding with excitement. Oh, she could not wait to tell Jane and Louise. In addition, she would have to call Mark, of course, and

Ellen and the twins. She would enclose a note to Joe with the foster care application. "Thank you so much. How would Sunday be for a first visit? I would do it sooner, but my family is deeply involved in a crafts fair this weekend and we all are a bit overwhelmed right now."

⟞

At long last, the Saturday of the first Grace Chapel Crafts Fair arrived. All day long, people streamed in and out, examining everything and buying, buying, buying.

Louise, dressed in practical khaki slacks and a checked blouse that was her idea of casual wear, met Alice in the middle of the Assembly Room shortly before three.

Alice's nose was a bit pink, and she rubbed her gloved hands together. She wore a long-sleeved blue sweater over her favorite jeans and she carried a heavy coat. Ethel had recruited her to work outdoors selling hot chocolate and cider, so Alice had been outside much of the day. "It is really chilly out there. At first I didn't think it was too bad, but that wind cuts right through me."

"That is a shame," Louise said. "I know Aunt Ethel had hoped that her outdoor ideas would be a popular draw."

"Oh, they have been," Alice assured her. "We sold out of hot chocolate about an hour ago, and the last of the cider just went, which is why I am free. My duties are officially completed." She gestured toward the doors. "So many people attended the carding and spinning demonstrations that next year I think we should offer more than one of each. How has it gone in here?"

Louise shrugged. "About as I expected. A few small squabbles over square inches, but generally everyone has been polite and helpful. They are happy because they sold a great deal of their wares." She rocked a little, trying to give her aching feet a break. "Attendance was astounding."

Alice looked around. "It looks like a flock of crows picked this field clean."

Louise laughed. "That might be more accurate than you think!"

Tables covered in white cloths were set up all over the room, creating small niches into which different vendors had shown their craft offerings. Tall racks bore baskets, ornaments, scarves and more, but there was plenty of white space atop the tables and on the racks where vendors had run out of items to be sold. The entire space had hummed with bustling people all day long, and only now was it beginning to empty out.

Along one wall were two long tables. One displayed the raffle items Jane and Sylvia had solicited. Sylvia still sat there, animatedly chatting with people purchasing tickets. The other table had been covered in tasty-looking baked goods. There was a mad rush to purchase those, and the very last brownie had been sold more than an hour ago.

Jane, looking positively exhausted, joined them a moment later.

"I'm glad this crafts fair is going to be over today," Louise remarked. "I'm not sure you could take another week of this pace."

"Oh, it's my own fault," Jane told her. She was wearing baggy brown corduroy overalls with an ivory turtle-necked blouse. "I stayed up until almost three in the morning baking."

"Oh, Jane, whatever for? You already did so much that I'm sure baked goods were not necessary."

"I wanted to do it." Jane grinned. "I'm bleary-eyed and weaving on my feet, but I've performed a true labor of love."

"You're a saint." Louise clasped her hands together as though she were at prayer.

"So are you. I heard you tell Aunt Ethel you would walk around, answer the vendors' questions and mediate any disagreements over space. That could not have been a fun job."

"Hello, girls!" Ethel rushed up, a pencil stuck behind one ear and a notebook in her hand. Her freshly tinted hair glowed like a beacon, making her easy to spot. "Thank you all for your help. Alice, I know supervising the outside activities meant you were out in that wind all day, but there simply was no one else I would have wanted in that position. Louise, I appreciate all your suggestions. They certainly made this day run far more smoothly than it would have had I fumbled through it on my own. And Jane, dear, I know that most of the credit for the success of this goes to all the hard work you and Sylvia did. I have prayed for the success of this venture, and I think God did a wonderful job of choosing the right people to help me."

"Florence helped too," Jane added. "Don't forget Florence, Aunt Ethel."

"Well, of course I would not forget Florence," Ethel huffed. "As a matter of fact, last night, I asked her if she would be interested in cochairing the event with me next year. That way, you wouldn't have such a burden," she said to Jane. "I confess I didn't quite realize when I asked you to chair crafts that it would be such an all-consuming task, and I feel bad about that. Dear Louise helped around the inn in Alice's absence, I know, but—What?" she demanded.

All three of her nieces were staring at her as if she had grown a second head.

"What?" she said again.

"Did you say you asked Florence to cochair?" Jane's jaw dropped.

"Why, yes. Oh!" Ethel looked aghast. "Has that hurt your feelings, Jane? I am so sorry I did not ask you first. I just assumed that you would rather not be in charge again next year." Ethel looked truly distressed. "I am trying so hard to be more sensitive to other people's feelings. I have never considered a lack of tact to be one of my failings, but this experience has shown me that on rare occasions I fail to recognize when I am being high-handed."

There was a silence.

"Indeed," Louise finally managed.

"Well, in any event, if you want the job, Jane, of course it is yours. I'm sure Florence would understand."

"No. No!" said Jane hastily. "Florence is wonderfully suited for the crafts chairmanship. I think she will do a fine job."

Ethel consulted her notebook. "I must fly! I will talk to you later, girls."

Alice thought of Joe MacAfell, the Camp Compassion director, with his ever-present clipboard. Nostalgia washed through her, but her longing to drop everything and return to Florida had receded. She was necessary here. At the hospital, at the inn and with her family.

When Alice had decided to travel south, God opened a door and offered her a new path to tread, and she accepted eagerly. Nevertheless, she knew His present plans for her included sharing her life with her two sisters and aunt, as well as with many others.

She tuned in to the conversation to see Louise shaking her head and Jane laughing.

"I will never forget that," said Jane, almost doubled over. She quoted, "'I have never considered a lack of tact to be one of my failings.' That might be the funniest thing I have ever heard."

"'On rare occasions I fail to recognize when I am being high-handed.'" Louise was chuckling now too. "I'm going to cross-stitch that onto a sampler so that the next time Aunt Ethel and I go head-to-head, I can read it and refrain from getting angry."

"What makes you think there will be a next time?" Alice asked.

Louise and Jane looked at each other, then back at their dear, idealistic sister. "There will be!" they said in unison.

About the Author

Anne Marie Rodgers has published nearly three dozen novels since 1992, has been a finalist for the prestigious RITA award and has won several Golden Leaf awards, among others. In addition, she has been a teacher of handicapped and preschool children, has been involved in animal-rescue efforts for many years, and has raised puppies for Guiding Eyes for the Blind. Anne Marie and her family live in State College, Pennsylvania.

Tales from Grace Chapel Inn

Back Home Again
by Melody Carlson

Recipes & Wooden Spoons
by Judy Baer

Hidden History
by Melody Carlson

Ready to Wed
by Melody Carlson

The Price of Fame
by Carolyne Aarsen

We Have This Moment
by Diann Hunt

The Way We Were
by Judy Baer

The Spirit of the Season
by Dana Corbit

The Start of Something Big
by Sunni Jeffers

Spring Is in the Air
by Jane Orcutt

Home for the Holidays
by Rebecca Kelly

Eyes on the Prize
by Sunni Jeffers

Tempest in a Teapot
by Judy Baer

Summer Breezes
by Jane Orcutt

Mystery at the Inn
by Carolyne Aarsen

Once you visit the charming village of Acorn Hill, you'll never want to leave. Here, the three Howard sisters reunite after their father's death and turn the family home into a bed and breakfast. They rekindle old memories, rediscover the bonds of sisterhood, revel in the blessings of friendship and meet many fascinating guests along the way.

～